A White House Friendship Begins

MARY LINCOLN INTERVIEWED dressmakers to make her lavish gowns. But all those she hired she was displeased with. Fashion was of prime importance to her. On one particular occasion she wanted a "bright rose-colored moiré antique gown," and determined to find just the right dressmaker, she set out to interview three or four more.

Early one morning at the beginning stages of the presidency, a light-skinned black woman walked up to the front entrance of the White House. She wanted the position of dressmaker to the First Lady but didn't think she had a chance of getting it.

Already successful in her trade, and the favorite of Washington's elite, she was a free black woman who had purchased her own freedom.

The interview lasted only a few minutes, and in that time Mary Lincoln hired the free black woman.

Her name was Elizabeth Keckley.

An Unlikely Friendship

OTHER NOVELS BY ANN RINALDI

Ann Rinaldi

An Unlikely Friendship

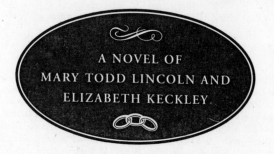

A NOVEL OF
MARY TODD LINCOLN AND
ELIZABETH KECKLEY

HARCOURT, INC.
Orlando Austin New York San Diego London

Requests for permission to make copies of any part of the work should be
submitted online at www.harcourt.com/contact or mailed to the following address:
Permissions Department, Houghton Mifflin Harcourt Publishing Company,
6277 Sea Harbor Drive, Orlando, Florida 32887-6777.

www.HarcourtBooks.com

First Harcourt paperback edition 2008

The Library of Congress has cataloged the hardcover edition as follows:
Rinaldi, Ann.
An unlikely friendship: a novel of Mary Todd Lincoln and
Elizabeth Keckley/Ann Rinaldi.
p.   cm.—(Harcourt great episodes)
Summary: Relates the lives of Mary Todd Lincoln, raised in a wealthy Virginia family,
and Lizzy Keckley, a dressmaker born a slave, as they grow up separately then become
best friends when Mary's childhood dream of living in the White House comes true.
1. Lincoln, Mary Todd, 1818–1882—Juvenile fiction. 2. Keckley, Elizabeth, ca. 1818–1907—
Juvenile fiction. [1. Lincoln, Mary Todd, 1818–1882—Fiction. 2. Keckley, Elizabeth, ca.
1818–1907—Fiction. 3. Slavery—Fiction. 4. Friendship—Fiction. 5. United States—
History—19th century—Fiction.] I. Title. II. Series.
PZ7.R459Unl   2007
[Fic]—dc22   2005030210
ISBN 978-0-15-205597-4
ISBN 978-0-15-206398-6 pb

Text set in Adobe Garamond
Designed by Cathy Riggs

DOM 10 9 8 7 6 5 4 3 2
4500293032

Printed in the United States of America

An Unlikely Friendship is a work of fiction based on historical figures and events.
Some details have been altered to enhance the story.

*To Mr. Paul, who helps me out
with all my disasters with the computer*

An Unlikely Friendship

Prologue
Friday, April 14, 1865

"Tad, give me that rebel flag."

"I won't, Wobert. It's mine."

Coming down the hallway in the family residence of the White House, Mary Lincoln heard her two sons arguing before she got to the dining room.

"Do you think," Robert asked, "that it's right to be waving a rebel flag around here when the war is just over?"

"It's been over for five whole days," Tad answered. At twelve, Taddy could not read or write, was just learning to say his *r*'s, but was smart enough for two. His tutor taught him by reading to him, by telling him things. He learned by talking to everyone who crossed his path. By listening. He was their baby.

"Where did you get it, anyway?" Robert demanded. "Who around here has rebel flags? Tell me and I'll tell father." Robert, the older by ten years, was just back from the front last night, from Appomattox Court House. An aide to General U. S. Grant, he'd been present at the surrender of General Lee.

"Won't tell where I got it," Tad said firmly. "And I know where to get more, too, if you take it fwom me."

"Not going to take it from you, you poor little begger," Robert said. "I'll let Father do that."

"He won't, either. Didn't he have the army band play 'Dixie' last night? Didn't he?"

"Boys, boys." Mary Lincoln swept into the sun-filled family dining room in her white cashmere morning sacque. Both boys rose as she entered and she kissed them, one after another. "Don't fuss. Remember, today is Good Friday and a day of thanksgiving in the North as proclaimed by your father. A day of peace. Robert, did you sleep well?"

"No, Mother. I'm not used to sleeping in a bed. These last few weeks Grant's staff has been sleeping all over the place. On the ground, on porches."

"You poor dear." She sat as he held out her chair. He was her darling boy, more handsome than ever now in his captain's uniform. Oh, she'd been proud of him when he'd gone off to Exeter to study, then Harvard. But now, home from the war, even with a three-day beard on his face, he was more precious than ever.

Not that he'd actually *gone off to war* these last few years. His "enlistment" had been recent, but only because she'd begged her husband not to let him go. Robert even had wanted to go back in Harvard. It was public criticism that had finally made her relent, and so her husband pulled some strings and had got Robert on General Grant's staff. But she was proud of him nevertheless.

"Where's Pa?" Tad asked petulantly.

"He'll be along directly," Robert said. "He has a cabinet meeting. Mother, do I have to go to the theater with you both tonight?"

"Everybody expects us, dear. The play is *Our American Cousin.*"

"I thought you saw that already," Robert reminded her.

"We did. But your father likes the humor. And I'd say he needs all the humor he can get these days."

"Well, I'm going to have to beg off. I'm just too tired, Mother."

"Of course, darling."

Over her shoulder James, who served at table, poured her steaming coffee into a delicate china cup. The table was set with the good sterling, crystal, and china she'd purchased from the New York importers E. V. Haughwout. With its imported Irish linen cloth, the table looked lovely.

James served her eggs, bacon, and then some fresh fish and biscuits before he passed the steaming platters to Robert, who helped Tad.

"Are General Grant and his wife going with you?" Robert asked.

"Your father invited them, but they declined. I don't think Julia Grant likes me," she told him.

"Now Mother," Robert chided, "don't say that."

"No, Mother, don't." He came into the room, rubbing his hands together briskly, a tall man in black trousers and black frock coat. He bent over, kissing her. And he smelled of his shaving cream and lemon. "Good morning, everyone."

"Good morning, Papa." The boys stood. Robert called him "sir." And then all proceeded to eat.

"Father, you've got to ask Tad where he got the rebel flag," Robert persisted.

"By jings, so he does have one. Simon, my valet, told me and I didn't believe it. Where did you get it, son?" Abraham Lincoln asked.

"Fwom someone in the army band," Tad confessed.

"The army band!" his father exclaimed. "So we have a traitor amongst us." And he laughed.

"You gonna take it fwom me?" Tad's lips quivered.

"Well," Abraham Lincoln allowed, "it doesn't look so good for a son of the President of the United States to go running around with a Confederate flag now, does it?"

"You got a picture of Genewal Lee. Wobert gave it to you. I heard about it."

Abraham Lincoln laughed. "By jings, I think I'll bring you into a cabinet meeting," he said. Then, "What's wrong, Mary? Don't fret. Senator Ira Harris's daughter, Clara, and her fiancé, Major Henry Rathbone, will come to the theater with us tonight."

"It isn't that," Mary said. "I have a headache." She didn't tell him that sometimes her vision got blurry, too. That it had been this way for two weeks now, ever since she'd fallen out of her carriage and hit her head on a rock, coming home from their summer retreat, the Soldiers' Home, where she'd gone to oversee some repairs.

"You should rest this afternoon then," he told her.

"I've a fitting this morning with Lizzy Keckley," she said, "for my dress for tonight. And you and I are going for a carriage ride this afternoon, remember? I've got to get you away from here or the hordes of people will eat you alive."

"I'd be poor pickins'." He chuckled.

"Wobert, tell us about the suwwender," Tad said.

"I told Father last night."

"Tell me and Mama then."

"Yes, tell us, do, dear." In spite of her headache, Mary's eyes beamed.

"Well, I'll tell you some of it," Robert said. "They used the McLean house. It was the nicest place in Appomattox Court House."

"What was Lee like?" Tad begged.

"All spiffed up. All dandified," Robert told them. "He wore a new gray uniform, with polished buttons and a wonderful sword with jewels in the hilt. And his spurs looked like silver."

"I hear he's a handsome man," Mary said.

"He's the enemy," Tad said.

"No, son," his father told him solemnly. "He is no longer the enemy. The war is over. We must be friends now. We're all Americans."

Tad grimaced, but Robert went on.

"Grant, on the other hand, wore his usual blue uniform. It had nothing but shoulder straps to designate his rank. I tried to get the jacket from him that morning, to brush it off, but he wouldn't let me. I tried to get him to have his orderly shine his boots, but he said no. He had no spurs." Robert shook his head sadly. "He wouldn't hear of any of it."

"He didn't need all the show," Tad said. "He won."

"That's right, son," his father told him. "He won. Now how would you like to make a bargain with me?"

Tad eyed him suspiciously.

"How would you like to go to Grover's Theater this afternoon with your tutor and see *The Wonderful Lamp*, a play about Aladdin's lamp?"

"What do I have to do?" Tad asked.

"Give me that Confederate flag," his father coaxed.

Tad studied on the matter for a few minutes, then finally pushed the small flag across the white tablecloth to his father. "I always wanted to see that play," he said.

"Well, I have my appointment with Lizzy Keckley," Mary said.

The three men stood as she pushed back her chair and swept from the room.

IN HER DRESSING ROOM Mary allowed Lizzy Keckley to slip the taffeta gown over her head and adjust it as it fell to the floor. "Remember the first summer you sewed for me, Lizzy?" Mary asked. "You made me fifteen or sixteen dresses."

"I remember," Lizzy said through a mouthful of pins. She took them out of her mouth and knelt to pin up the hem, working her way around the bottom of the dress while kneeling on the floor. "And after that you never made me do any plain sewing again. No more darning, mending, or patching." She giggled, remembering.

"Well, Mary Ann, the Irish servant I hired in New York to take care of all that, turned out well, don't you think?"

"I certainly do, ma'am."

"Until now I thought the white silk you made for me for the second inauguration was the best you ever did,"

Mary told her. "But now that I see this, I've changed my mind. You've outdone yourself with this, Lizzy." And she whirled around in front of the full-length mirror, admiring the black taffeta with the tiny white flowers, the scooped neck with the beribboned ruffle, and even the lace head-piece Lizzy had made for the top of her hair. "I don't look fat in this dress," she pronounced.

"You never look fat," Lizzy assured her.

"You know what Mr. Lincoln is going to say about this dress, don't you, Lizzy? He's going to say, 'Our cat has a long tail tonight.'"

They both laughed. Lizzy stood, her pinning finished. "I'll sew up that hem this afternoon," she said.

The two women beamed at each other for a few seconds. The look carried across over four years of intimate friendship now.

"You've always been there for me," Mary said. "For us. You were with us when my baby Willie died. Through that nightmare I don't know what I would have done without you. And afterward, during the terrible months of mourning. You got me a spiritualist for the séances we had right here at the White House. They helped me. Oh, they did, Lizzy."

"And you were there for me when my son was killed in the war," Lizzy returned.

"Yes, and now this." Mary sighed. "Now the war is over."

"Yes, ma'am. Now the war is over."

"Your people are free, Lizzy."

"Yes."

"When I was a child, do you know what my Mammy Sally said to me when I told her I never wanted to leave her?" Mary asked. "She said, 'you'll find yourself another Mammy Sally, don't you worry.' And that's what you've been for me, Lizzy. A Mammy Sally. And more than that, a true friend."

Lizzy knelt to adjust a ruffle at the bottom of the dress. "Better stitch this up, this afternoon, or it'll fall and you'll trip on it," she said. "Don't want any accidents at Ford's Theater tonight."

"And now what, I wonder," Mary said wistfully, "now that the war is over."

"Now you all will finish your term in the White House," practical Lizzy said, "and, Lord willin', I'll be with you."

"Why, of course you will be, Lizzy. I couldn't go it without you."

Lizzy looked up. Then she stood. As if on cue, the two women, one who'd been a slave for years, the other who'd grown up as a pampered Kentucky darling, hugged.

Lizzy drew away first and wiped a tear from her eye. "I wonder, ma'am," she said.

"Yes?"

"I wonder what's going to happen to that General Lee now that the war's over."

"He'll be fine. My husband is practicing clemency toward the South."

"In October of '60, before I knew you, I made a dress for his wife. Everyone liked it so much I got important ladies like Mrs. Jeff Davis for my clients. And that General

Lee was awful kind to me. 'Course, he wasn't a general yet. But he was so kind! I won't forget it."

"Of course you won't. And you shouldn't."

"You can take the dress off now, ma'am. I'll have it ready for tonight. And I'll be here to fix your hair, too. Your head hurt again?"

"Yes, Lizzy. Most terrible."

"You sit down and rest. And I'll get you a laudanum. There you go. Lizzy'll take care of that head for you. You'll see."

THE LINCOLNS' BAROUCHE, pulled by a matching set of black horses and driven by their man, Jacob, made its way steadily down Pennsylvania Avenue, which was still full of people celebrating the end of the war.

They drove under triumphal arches decorated with flowers. The fire of gasoline torchlights was everywhere. Some of the paraders were doing victory dances.

"The last time we were at Ford's Theater we saw *Martha,*" Mary reminded her husband. "And before that we saw John Wilkes Booth in *The Marble Heart.*"

"None are as humorous as this one," he allowed.

"Oh, I think you just like the star, Laura Keene."

"She is a pretty one all right. But you know, Mother, it wouldn't have taken me much to stay home tonight. And be quiet with a beautiful lady like you."

"Except that it wouldn't be quiet," she reminded him. "The place is full of favor seekers. How many favors did you grant today, Abraham?"

He was quiet for a moment. "The last one would inter-est you. A mother of a young Northern boy, a deserter who was sentenced to be shot, came to me. She was from New York. A nice, plain woman. She begged me to pardon him. He was Robert's age."

"And did you?"

"I did, Mother. I figured, the war is over. We lost enough Roberts on both sides. Let him go home and be a productive citizen. Anyway, he's his mother's mainstay."

Mary put her hand on her husband's arm. "And he'll al-ways have you to thank for his life," she said.

THEIR BAROUCHE MADE its way down the cobblestoned streets to a brick Georgian house, the front of which was aglow with gaslight. There they picked up Clara Harris and Major Rathbone, both handsome enough and high enough in Washington society as to please Mary Lincoln.

They went on to Tenth Street, between E and F, and the barouche stopped outside the canopied front door of Ford's Theater. Mr. Ford's brother came out to meet them and a valet helped Mary down from the carriage and es-corted them into the theater and up to the presidential box.

They were half an hour late and the play had already started, but the actors and actresses paused so the band could play "Hail to the Chief." Seventeen hundred people in the theater cheered and applauded. President Lincoln took off his stovepipe hat and waved it, and Mary settled her taffeta skirts into a plush chair next to the president's rocker.

The presidential box was decorated with red, white,

and blue bunting and Nottingham lace curtains. As the second act started, the place got drafty.

"Put on your overcoat, dear," Mary told her husband.

"Do you think it would be proper?"

"Of course. You mustn't catch cold. We have the most exciting times coming."

"We do, don't we?" He got up and put on his overcoat. In doing so he noticed that the guard sent to protect them had seated himself in the anteroom. But he said nothing, and let the man enjoy the play.

As he sat down again, he took Mary's hand. "As soon as my second term is up, we're going to make that trip to Europe you always wanted," he whispered. "Then we'll go back to Illinois and I'll reopen my law office. And we'll live happily ever after. Maybe Robert will come with us and practice law with me. And you can be the Queen of Springfield or Chicago or wherever we go."

She gazed up at him adoringly. "Oh, Abraham." She hugged his arm and rested her head on his shoulder. "I've never been so happy."

MARY DIDN'T KNOW which sound she heard first, the scream of a woman or the loud bang, which was like a firecracker. It was well into the third act, and she thought, *Firecrackers aren't part of the play.* Then she saw her husband's head slump forward, felt someone brush past her, and suddenly the form of a man holding a derringer stood poised before her on the railing of the box, half hidden by the Nottingham lace curtains.

"Stop that man! Stop him!" It was Major Rathbone's voice, shouting, as he threw himself at the dark form.

"Abraham! Abraham!" Mary shouted. "Oh, and they have shot my husband!"

She saw blood dripping from the back of Abraham's head, through the dark hair. His eyes were open but glassy. He could not see or hear her.

"Someone help us!" she pleaded. "Someone!"

Major Rathbone and the dark stranger were wrestling now, right in front of her. She saw a knife flash then heard a low moan from Rathbone. Then the stranger jumped from the box onto the stage below, dragging some lace curtain and red, white, and blue bunting with him.

The audience below was in a panic. The presidential box was full of people. Someone ushered Mary out. Doctors were there now, laying her husband down on the carpet. Laura Keene, the lead actress, was there. Clara Harris was sobbing and begging a doctor to see to her fiancé's arm, which was bleeding profusely.

Then they carried Abraham out. Strangers were helping, Mary noted. They carried him downstairs, outside, and across the street to the Petersen house. There they set him down on a too-small bed in a too-small bedroom.

Mary stood dumbly, looking around while people pushed past her. Important people like members of the cabinet. How had they gotten here so suddenly? Wasn't that Secretary of War Edwin M. Stanton? She blinked. Gaslight flickered. Long shadows were cast on the wall. People spoke in low tones. Yet she could hear Abraham's labored breathing.

Able to abide it no more she wedged herself between all the important men and threw herself on Abraham. "Oh husband, husband, don't leave me like this!"

But Abraham was not responding. Of a sudden his cheeks looked sunken in. His eyes were unseeing, there and not there. Blood stained the pillowcase under his head. "Do something," she scolded the doctors. "Can't you do something?"

"Someone get that woman out of here!" It was Secretary Stanton's voice. Oh well, she had never liked the man anyway, nor had he liked her. But always he had treated her with the deference of her position.

Now she had no more position. If Abraham died, no one would treat her with deference; she would be a nobody. The thought seized her, and she felt that fear piled onto the other.

"Mother, come. Come into the other room with me."

It was Robert. She turned and he stood there, tall and a boy no longer; he was a man now. If the war hadn't done it to him, this would. She took his hand, and he led her across the hall to a small gaslit parlor. People left them alone there. Robert sat next to her on the sofa. She suddenly saw tears brimming in his eyes and held him close. He needed her as much as she needed him.

"Who did this thing to your father?" she asked him. "Did they find out?"

"A man named John Wilkes Booth. The actor."

She shook her head. "No, no, it couldn't be. We saw him once in a play. Why would he? Why? Is he a Southern sympathizer?"

"No one knows the why of it yet, Mother."

"Did they catch him?"

"Not yet. No. But they will. They're all looking for him."

"The dream," she told Robert. "It's your father's dream. He told me of it within the last week. Do you want to know what he dreamed?"

"Becalm yourself, Mother. Here, I'll get you some brandy." He got up and went to a small table where there was a brandy set. He poured some in a glass and brought it to his mother.

"He told me he dreamed he awoke in his bed to the sound of people crying. He betook himself below stairs and there he saw, in the East Room, a corpse lying on a catafalque, surrounded by soldiers on guard. 'Who is dead in the White House?' he asked one of the soldiers. 'The president,' came the answer. 'He was killed by an assassin.' Then, sweating and shaking, he woke up. And he couldn't sleep the rest of the night."

"Mother, you must becalm yourself."

Mary looked around the small room. "Someone is missing, Robert."

"Who? Everyone is here. Except Tad. I didn't want to wake him."

"No, Lizzy. I want Lizzy Keckley, Robert. You must send a carriage for her." Mary was becoming agitated. "Please, Robert, send a carriage for her now. I must have Lizzy with me. I cannot endure this without her, Robert."

———

THE NOISE OUTSIDE on Twelfth Street did not waken Lizzy Keckley that night. She slept undisturbed until the knock came on the door at eleven o'clock. She got up, put on her robe, and went to the door before the knocking could wake the Lewises, her landlords.

It was a neighbor, Mrs. Brown. She looked desperate. "Mr. Lincoln has been shot," she told Lizzy.

At first she thought Mrs. Brown was drunk. Over her shoulder she saw revelers in the street, still celebrating the end of the war. But wait, they were not celebrating.

There were soldiers all about, with drawn bayonets, and the people—men, women, and children—were in nightclothes, some of them, and seemed to be wandering around aimlessly. They were wailing, sobbing. Some men were putting the flags at half-mast.

"Where?" she asked Mrs. Brown. "Who shot him?"

"I heard an actor by the name of John Wilkes Booth. The army is out looking for him now."

She drew in her breath sharply. Mrs. Lincoln! She must go to her. But go where? The play must be over by now. To the White House! "I must dress," she told herself. The night had grown chilly and there would be rain. "I must go now."

Within ten minutes she was out on Twelfth Street, pushing her way through the crowds of milling people. "Who shot him?" someone said. Then, "There's a reward of twenty thousand dollars for the murderers."

And, "Excuse me, ma'am, but you're colored, aren't you? All the colored people are assembling in front of the White House."

"Thank you," Lizzy said, and made her way toward the familiar mansion, walking briskly. Already soldiers were marching to the barking of orders; men were tearing down the flowers from light poles and putting up draped black bunting.

But oh, the crowd in front of the White House! She would never get through! She would go the back way, a way familiar to her, through alleys and shanties of the colored people. But it was dangerous going alone this time of night. She would go back to the house and get her landlords, the Lewises, to accompany her. Mr. Lewis was a big, brawny man and had a gun.

They were awake when she got back, throwing questions at her as they pulled on rain clothes, and she told them what it was like outside. "I can get us to the White House the way I know, but I can't go it alone," she told them.

They agreed to come with her. Mr. Lewis put his gun inside his oilcloth slicker and picked up and lighted a lantern. And once again she ventured out, this time feeling confident that she would get there.

By now it was quarter of one in the morning but it was like daylight in the streets, what with torchlight and bells tolling and army wagons rushing along and people gathering in bunches to console one another. All the windows of the houses were lighted, and there was an angry murmuring in the crowds.

Lizzy led the Lewises the back way, away from the crowds, through the alleyways, and along the paths that she knew. She could smell the Potomac River as they rushed along past hovels and huts of the poor, with the rain beating down on them now. Milk wagons and mail carts rushed past them, only to be turned back at the first corner by soldiers.

Finally they came to a great open space and saw the back of the White House looming up before them, like a giant birthday cake about to melt in the rain. Lights shone from all the windows. Lizzy opened a gate on the far end of the grounds and led the Lewises past the carriage house, the horse stables, the pen where Tad's pet goats were housed.

But there was another gate to go through now. And, as she feared, armed soldiers were guarding it. Oh well, they would know her. All the guards did.

"Halt there, identify yourselves."

Rifles with bayonets attached to the ends were pointed at them. A large lantern cast its light in their eyes, blinding them.

"I'm Elizabeth Keckley, Mrs. Lincoln's dressmaker. I'm here to help her. She'll need me."

One of the guards, a tall soldier with a Yankee twang, approached her. She didn't know him, didn't recognize any of them. Oh, this was bad.

"Who are these other people?" he asked.

"My landlords. The Lewises. Responsible people. We live on Twelfth Street."

"I don't care where you live, lady," another one of them said as he stepped forward. "The president's been shot this night and is near death. We're letting nobody in. And one thing's certain: Mrs. Lincoln isn't going to need any dressmaker tonight. No sir. So you just take yourself and your responsible friends and go home and stitch a fine seam."

They were treating her like a nobody! How could she make them understand? Inside her heart was breaking. Mary would be looking for her, expecting her. How could she explain? She couldn't. She was just another of hundreds of colored women to these war-weary soldiers. Just another threat on a nightmare of a night.

"Come on, let's go," she told her friends. And the three of them turned and left.

MEANWHILE, THE CARRIAGE and driver Robert had dispatched to fetch Elizabeth Keckley in her house on Twelfth Street was searching and searching for her, but the driver got lost, what with the crowds, the armed soldiers, and the stopping and searching of each carriage on the streets.

So Mary Lincoln had to go back to the White House alone that terrible rainy morning after they pronounced her husband dead.

As she left the lodging house on Tenth Street, a doctor was putting silver dollars on Lincoln's eyelids. "Oh, that dreadful, dreadful place," she was saying of Ford's Theater. "That horrible place."

Apparently others felt the same, for crowds gathering on Tenth Street were already shouting "Burn it down, burn it," at Ford's Theater.

As she climbed into the carriage, a group of people were carrying a long coffin down the steps of the Petersen house. A group of army officers followed the coffin, bareheaded, back to the White House. Robert Lincoln followed on his horse.

In the White House Mary Lincoln wandered around upstairs aimlessly. She could not bring herself to go into any of the familiar bedrooms. She wrung her hands and cried. Her head pounded. She needed Lizzy Keckley. Oh, where was Lizzy? Mammy Sally had always been around when she needed her. Where was Lizzy?

Finally she allowed two friends, Elizabeth Dixon and Mary Jane Welles, to put her to bed in a small, unused room.

She cried all through the early rainy morning, hearing the crowds outside on Pennsylvania Avenue, listening to the church bells toll, seeing lights and shadows cast on the flowered wallpaper. Robert came and went, gave her a powder and some water. She finally dozed, and when she awoke on that Saturday morning, she gave the order again.

"Go and get my friend Elizabeth Keckley. She is the only one who understands me."

Mary Todd

Lexington, Kentucky

I HAVE LONG SINCE learned not to believe idle stories. Heaven knows I grew up on them. For years as a child I was terrorized by family stories of great Uncle John being killed at Blue Licks by Indians. Or how Uncle John escaped from Indians after running a gauntlet and his brother Sam was captured and Uncle John ransomed him for a barrel of whiskey.

Not to mention Mammy Sally's stories about Jaybird reporting once a week to the Almighty about our misdoings for which, somehow, we'd be punished. Jaybird reported only to God, she said.

But for some reason I did believe the rumor told to me by my sisters Frances and Elizabeth of how, only weeks after our mother's burial, our father was courting another woman.

I believe it because my older sisters were friends with Dr. Warfield's daughter, Claire. And he'd been in attendance at my mother's death and was a friend of my father.

They tell me this woman is from Frankfort, the state capital where my father goes frequently because he is a state senator. They say she has a seventy-three-year-old mother who is the head of society there. That she herself wants to be called Betsy, and that she hopes to lift our family to new standards of elegance.

Grandmother Parker, who lives just up the hill from us here in Lexington and is my own mother's ma, says it is an indecently short time after Ma's death for Pa to go courting.

My sister Frances says Pa sent his new lady a miniature of himself painted by Lexington's own Matthew Jouett.

Elizabeth Humphreys she is called. I made it my business to find out everything I could about her. She is no stranger to Lexington. Two of her uncles taught here at our Transylvania college.

She is going to bring her own black servants with her when she comes. I wonder how that will sit with Mammy Sally.

Jaybird can tell God all he wants about me. I know already that I do not like her.

IT WAS IN THE AIR a long time, this silent courtship of Pa's. Auntie Ann, his sister, who ran the household since Ma died, warned us not to ask him about it. So we didn't. But we watched him closely at the dinner table to see if he was changing toward us.

For all we could see, he wasn't.

He still asked Levi if he'd been a good boy that day and ruffled his hair when he asked it. He still told my spoiled sister Ann how pretty she was. He still discussed social matters with Elizabeth and Frances. And he still promised me a pony if I was a good girl. He'd been promising me a pony for ages. As long as he kept promising, I figured my hope for a pony was still alive. Though I did wonder if a pony would fit in with Betsy's idea of a new standard of elegance.

No, he wasn't changing toward us. He was still Pa, who loved us and wouldn't let anything come between us.

SOMETIME AROUND CHRISTMAS in 1825 my father called us all into the front parlor after dinner and cleared up the rumors. I was seven years old.

"My situation has become irksome," he said. "People of ill will are saying bad things about me and my intended, Elizabeth Humphreys. So I have become engaged to this dear lady and hope soon to wed. I need to complete my domestic circle so I can enjoy the repose and happiness which the world can never give."

Pa talked high words sometimes. But we understood. Frances and Elizabeth kissed him. I hugged him because I wasn't going to be left out of any part of his domestic circle.

THAT'S HOW WE LEARNED we were to get a stepmother. But I didn't see the need for one. As far as I was concerned, the domestic circle we had was complete enough. Mammy Sally ran the kitchen and the other servants. And I didn't see anything wrong with Auntie Ann running the house. She even did the male chores when Pa was away, oversaw the carriage, disciplined the servants, and bought the staples. Only bone I had to pick with her was that she favored my little sister Ann too much. Ann was the darling of her eye. I was almost eight the year Pa wed and Ann was going on two, and Ann took all the attention from me. Same as she'd taken my name when she was born. I was Mary Ann up until then, until they gave the second part of my name to her, and now I'm only Mary.

It's a lonely name, I can tell you. It needs a second part. Anybody can see that.

Elizabeth and Frances have their own set of fine-feathered girlfriends who can't talk about anything but dresses and boys. Levi, a year older than me, and George, only one at the time, had the full attention and love of Pa. All I had was Grandma Parker to stand up for me. And she was fifty-two.

I HAVE HAD A LOT of afflictions in my life, don't think that getting a stepmother was the first of them. Now that I am nineteen and about to leave Lexington, Kentucky, to live with my sister Elizabeth and her husband in Springfield, Illinois, I can write of them without hurting too much.

Before I was three years old I lost my place as the youngest in the family to brother Robert when he was born. When I was four I lost my baby brother. Robert died at fourteen months. I was uncommonly fond of Robert and his death affected me terribly. Then when I was five I lost part of my name. At seven I lost my mother when my next brother, George Rogers Clark Todd, was born.

At almost eight I got a new stepmother.

———

WE WERE TO CALL her "Ma" Pa told us in one of the most stern moments I ever recollect seeing him in. "Not *Betsy*, but *Ma*."

We all said yes.

"And if you have any concerns about the household, bring them to her. She wants to be in charge."

Concerns about the household? I'd had nothing but concerns since Auntie Ann had left us, as soon as Pa and Betsy came home from their wedding trip.

Concerns about the household? That phrase went through my mind as I stood in the kitchen and watched, transfixed, as Judy, one of Betsy's slaves, stood grim-faced, her two hands holding a large bowl of soup. I could smell the soup from where I stood. I loved that soup, all made with preserves from our garden.

Across the kitchen stood Mammy Sally, who had made the soup. She'd caught Judy sampling it from the serving bowl and scolded her.

"Here, take your ol' soup," Judy said and threw the bowl on the floor.

The smash of the china bowl sounded throughout the house. The soup splashed all over the place. I even got some on the hem of my dress. Mammy Sally backed away, held her hands to her face, and cried.

"Who wants your ol' soup." Judy stamped out of the kitchen.

Just then Pa appeared at the kitchen doorway. "What is this? What's going on here?"

"Judy threw the soup on the floor," I told him.

He looked shocked. I felt sorry for him. *So much for*

repose and happiness, I thought. And, as if he could read my thoughts, he looked at me. "Mary, go and get your mother," he said quietly. Then he turned and went back into his study.

For a moment I thought that he really meant my mother. The look on his face was so confused that for all I knew he could have been wanting her then, just like I was. But I ran upstairs to get Betsy.

She was seated at her dressing table, making up her hair. "What's all the noise?" she asked.

I just stood there like a jackass in the rain. "Ma," my voice cracked when I said it. "The servants are fighting. There won't be any soup for supper."

"And why is that?"

"Judy threw it on the floor."

"Well, she must have had provocation."

So that was the way it was to be. Her servants could do no wrong. "Pa needs you," I said.

She stood up. "Is there no order in this house?"

I shrugged. "Your Judy threw the soup when Mammy Sally found her eating out of the serving bowl."

"There must be more to it than that."

New standards of elegance, I thought.

"And you don't have to look so pained when you call me Ma, either. Now say it again. And say it strong."

I swallowed. "Ma," I said.

"Again."

Tears came to my eyes. "Ma."

She swept past me. "I hope I don't have to speak to your father about you. Now go and tell the others to come to the dinner table."

I walked past the kitchen to see Mammy Sally on her hands and knees cleaning up the soup.

"You didn't throw it." I stood there in the doorway on my way into supper. "Tell her to make Judy clean it up."

"Judy serving supper," Mammy said. "Anyways," and she raised herself up on her knees, "you knows what I tol' you, little one. No slave in this town is safe from bein' sold down the river. The trader be around alla' time. An' the slave pens be close at hand."

Even though no negro servant in our house was ever spoken to roughly, they all feared being sold down the river. To the rice swamps or the sugar or cotton plantations. They knew that any minute things could change for them. A death in the family, or a marriage, or a decline in the hemp prices could do it. Mammy Sally had explained it all to me. Even admitted she was afeared of Betsy.

I knew about slavery. You didn't grow up in Lexington without knowing about it. It was the chief discussion at every dinner party my father had when politicians gathered at the table. And we lived on Short Street, not far from the town square where, in the southwest corner, there was the black locust whipping post, ten feet high, from where you could hear the screams of the slave being whipped, if you couldn't see it. And every Monday morning when court was in session our slave auctions took place.

My pa didn't like slavery. He didn't believe in selling them, though he'd purchased Harvey for $700, Pendleton for $550, and Chaney and her small daughter and son came at a real bargain for $905. Pa was one of the men in town who wanted to send freed slaves to Liberia.

I knew by then that slavery was an explosive topic that affected everybody in my world. I knew that I loved Mammy Sally, that she had been my safe harbor since before Ma died, and that now I depended on her more than anything.

"Go in for supper," she said. "An' doan make trouble."

I obeyed. As I slid into my chair at the table, Betsy gave me a disapproving look. Judy set a bowl of mashed potatoes down in front of me, and Nelson, Pa's personal body servant and our carriage driver, winked at me as if we had some secret. He was standing over Pa, serving him wine.

"You're late," Pa observed.

"I was talking to Mammy."

"And I was telling about my niece, Elizabeth Humphreys. Do you think you could listen, Mary?" Betsy queried.

"She'd best, as she's to be Elizabeth's companion while she's here," my sister Frances said.

As it turned out, she was right. Elizabeth Humphreys was coming to live with us. She was to be called Liz, she was my age, and she was coming because of the good schools in Lexington. She was from Frankfort, and I was to share my room with her.

"You'll go to school together," Pa said.

"I don't go to school," I reminded him.

"You will. Next semester. You'll go to Ward's with Liz. She'll be a good friend."

I don't want a friend, I wanted to say. I want my ma back. I want you to love me, Pa. I want a pony to show you love me. I want a hoopskirt. I want to live in the White House someday. And I want your promise that you'll never sell Mammy or Nelson down the river.

We ate supper. The conversation took another turn. And Judy served.

I ALWAYS WANTED to live in the White House when I grew up. It was something I dreamed about the way other girls my age dreamed of marrying Prince Charming. Our neighbor and most prominent citizen, Senator Henry Clay, who wanted to be president, told me that when he lived there he'd invite me to visit. There wasn't a soul in Lexington who wanted him to be president more than I did.

THE REASON I'D NEVER BEEN to school was because in Lexington boys started at six or seven and girls at eight or nine. As it was I'd be almost nine when I started at Ward's in the fall. Only young people from important families went to Ward's, so my family must be important, in spite of what Pa's new wife had said to me last time she got angry.

"It takes seven generations to make a lady, Mary. You have a long way to go."

I didn't mind the insult to me. But I minded it to my family.

"My ancestors founded this town," I told her. "They named it Lexington after the town in New England where the war was started."

"That still doesn't make you a lady," she'd retorted.

That was yesterday, and today there was the business with the soup and Elizabeth Humphreys coming. She was trying to undo me all right, this lady. My spirit was brought low, exactly as she wanted.

It was time to go and visit Grandma Parker.

GRANDMA PARKER WAS OLD. She was all of fifty-two. She had five children, fifteen grandchildren, and seven slaves. But she was never too busy to see me and welcome me in her two-story brick house up the hill from us.

When my mother and father had wed, she'd given them the lower part of her lot so that our two houses looked like one compound. When my ma first married, she was taken over by running a home and often sought help from her mother. And then my pa was away a lot, visiting New Orleans to buy his French brandies, Holland gin, and green coffee that he and his partner in the dry goods business sold from their store to Lexington's carriage trade. In such times Grandma Parker sent her own slaves "down the hill" to help.

She kept a close eye on us, too, after Ma's death, eventually letting us keep Mammy Sally, who belongs to us now. I know she didn't approve of Betsy. And, while she didn't encourage us in our dislike for her, she didn't discourage us, either.

"Mary, come in, come in." She held open her arms and I quickly went into them, hugging her slender form tightly. "Child, child, what is it? Is she plaguing you again?"

"She said I'll never be a lady." I drew back and wiped my eyes. "She's always after me, like a fox after a bluebird."

"How are the others faring?"

"She's mean to us all. But mostly to me. She does it on the sly, so Pa doesn't hear or know."

"Of course she does. Here, would you like some tea?"

I said yes and she ordered one of her servants to fetch it, and before long we were sitting at the tea table in her elegant parlor and I was feeling better. I looked around the room. "Why can't I live here with you?" I asked for what was likely the twentieth time.

"Because your pa needs you."

I gave a bitter laugh. "Pa? Needs me?"

"Yes. He needs all of you." She poured tea out of a silver pot she'd once told me had been made by Paul Revere and handed down in her family. "Did you ever think how it would hurt him if you left?"

I hadn't.

"Besides, you *are* a lady. I wouldn't have you in my house if you weren't."

"She said it takes seven generations to make a lady."

"Then tell her about your grandfather Levi Todd's wife, Jane, who was living in a stockade in Kentucky when she wove her wedding dress from the weeds and wild flax that were the only materials she had. She may not have had frills and ruffles, but she was a lady."

I listened intently. Once Grandma Parker started on

family legends, she never stopped. But if you paid mind to her, at least she wouldn't go on forever.

"What do you need, child? Is there anything I can give you?"

"I want a hoopskirt," I said petulantly.

"Did you ask your stepmother?"

"Yes. She said I'm too young."

"Well, you are a mite young. But when the time comes, I'll help you make one."

She was an excellent seamstress, my grandmother. Together we had made several of my dresses. She paid for the fabric and the bows and ruffles. She was always giving me money for something.

Her home was beautiful and, with her white hair and lively blue eyes and chiseled features, she was beautiful, too. I was proud of her, proud to be part of everything she was. And she was the matriarch in town, known as the Widow Parker.

"Will you come and visit us sometime?" I asked when I left.

"I don't go down there anymore," she said. "Not since my daughter died. She is welcome to come and pay her respects to me anytime she wishes. Now remember what I told you. Tell her about Grandmother Jane and the woven wedding dress."

She hugged me when I left and pressed some coins into my hand. "Buy yourself a little something," she murmured into my ear.

My spirit soared when I left her.

———

BY LATE SPRING Liz Humphreys arrived with all the ceremony of a true Southern belle. The carriage bearing her was drawn by two horses and included a footman who put down the step with a flourish of a bow. Out stepped Liz, holding a froufrou of a puppy dog.

I'd wanted a dog after Mama died but Pa had said no. Liz intended to let this one not only live in the house but sleep in her bed. And Pa was fine with it.

Everyone greeted Liz with the good wishes they usually saved for politicians who stopped in Lexington on their way to Frankfort. She was done up in fine feathers too showy for our town. All ruffles and bows and golden beribboned curls under a velvet hat I would kill for.

She came with four more trunks of clothing. I hated her on sight. The only thing that kept me from jumping on her and pulling her hair was that she wasn't wearing a hoopskirt.

"MY ROOM AT HOME is bigger than this. But at least this isn't as bad as I expected."

"What did you expect, a wooden shack surrounded by savage Indians?"

She raised her chin. She was pretty. I had to give her that. "No. My mama told me you-all weren't that bad off." She plumped herself down on the bed and set the dog, Pierre, on the floor. I thought of my father's hunting dogs out back in the pen and how I'd always wanted a dog for a house pet.

"What do you do around here?" she asked.

"What people do anywhere. There's lots to do." I found myself defending Lexington.

"Is your daddy an important man?"

"He's a state senator. He knows everybody. My grandfathers started this town. Our best friend is Senator Henry Clay. He's going to run for president, and when he lives in the White House I'm going to be invited for a visit."

She eyed me unblinkingly. "My grandmother rules society in Frankfort. Every year she leads the procession in the ball. She wears a lace cap like aristocrats from the federal period. If she doesn't accept you in town, you're an outsider forever."

We sat, each on a bed, facing each other. I swung my foot. "I'm going to have a pony one of these days. My pa says so."

"Will you let me ride it?"

"If you behave."

She reached down and lifted Pierre onto her lap and hugged him close. "I didn't want to come here. My mama made me come. Do you have a hoopskirt?"

Something stirred inside me. "No."

"Neither do I. I'm not allowed. Mama says I'm too young. If I could make one, I'd make it myself."

"My Grandma Parker said she'll help me make one when the time comes."

"When is that?" She looked at me hopefully.

I thought about Grandma Parker. I assessed her love and decided I wouldn't be lying.

"Soon," I said. "And if you stop acting like a silly-boots she could help you make one, too."

Liz set Pierre back down, slipped off the bed, and offered her hand, just like a man would. I took it and we shook hands. "I'm really not a silly-boots," she said. "I was just so scared when I got here. Will you be my friend?"

We shook on that, too.

Liz was a hopeless case. I had to school her in everything. Most likely she'd associated too much with that grandmother of hers in the aristocratic lace cap.

First off, she was afraid of everything: garden snakes, the woods, lightning and thunder, turtles, bugs of all kinds, the peacocks that roamed around our house that my father used as watchdogs, and Mammy Sally.

Apparently she'd never been on friendly terms with a negro in Frankfort, and when Mammy Sally jokingly told her one day she was going to send Jaybird to scold her, she became terrified of Jaybird and all the other demons of Mammy Sally's negro world.

I must confess that I added to her fears. I couldn't resist telling her about the legend of the woods surrounding Lexington. On the Maysville Pike to the north was the thick underbrush of canebrake, peavine, and pawpaw. To the east were the large sycamores, maples, and wild cherries.

"The Cherokees called it a dark and bloody land," I

told her when we were lying awake in our beds one night. "Anything you can imagine lives in those woods."

"Like what?"

"Buffalo," I lied, "wolves and giant mammoths, runaway slaves and savage Indians."

"Do the Indians ever come to town?"

"No, but they watch us all the time."

She half believed me and half knew I was just entertaining her. But her fear of the savage Indians was very real.

One day a band of friendly Cherokee Indians came through town, right past our windows. I ran to find Liz, to show her how friendly they appeared, but couldn't find her. Her screams led me to the cellar, where I found her hidden in a corner, praying and sobbing, "Don't let them get me. Don't let them scalp me, please."

I stopped feeding her fears after that. I didn't know that my tales of folklore, which I'd learned from Mammy Sally, were so effective.

THERE WAS NO PLACE in our family, Pa said, for ignorant women. So in September, the best time of the year, the time when the sunshine was so mellow you wanted to drink it and the sky so blue you wanted a dress of the same color, Liz and I trudged three blocks up the hill to Reverend and Mrs. Ward's school at the corner of Second and Market.

"I thought we were going to the Lafayette Female Academy," Liz said. "That's what my mama told me."

"We can't."

"Why?"

"The *Kentucky Gazette* said that the school lost its respectability. That emulation slept and virtue fled."

"What's emulation?"

"I don't know."

"Oh, Mary, look at that." She stood there staring.

I looked. It was a coffle of slaves, all manacled together, being led, groaning and shuffling, down the street.

"Where are they taking them?" Liz asked.

I stared, too. "To the flatboats in Louisville, to be taken downriver to the markets in New Orleans," I recited carefully. Pa had told me all about it. Pa was a secret abolitionist, I think, but he dared not speak such sentiments in Lexington.

"We're going to be late for school, Liz," I said. "Let's go."

I supposed she didn't see such sights in Frankfort. Or at least she had been kept from them. She insisted on staying and staring until the slaves were out of sight. And we were late for school on the first day. Reverend Ward was not happy. And that's when we found out what emulation meant.

"It means looking up to and trying to imitate the virtues, the character, and the values of our American heroes," Reverend Ward said solemnly as we stood before him, waiting for permission to go to class. "It means trying to be better than you are. Now, so as you learn, you will both stay after school today and write a paper about who, in our history or in your family, you would like to emulate. Understood?"

I don't know who Liz wrote about. Likely her grandmother with the lace cap. I wrote about how Grandma

Parker's maternal grandmother had brought food and clothing to her husband at Valley Forge. How she frequently brought provisions to the men and on one visit was greeted by General George Washington, who complimented her on her devotion to her husband and the cause.

When Reverend Ward read it, he scowled. "Where did you learn to write, Mary? Who taught you such words and such penmanship?"

"Sometimes my own mother," I said. "Sometimes Grandma Parker. Or Auntie Ann or my older sisters."

He harrumphed. "Good girl," he said begrudgingly. "Now go and sit and wait for your cousin. I think somehow that she has not had the same education as you."

It wasn't writing and penmanship that I had to learn at Ward's. Some of the other girls, like Margaret Wickliffe and Isabelle Trotter and one of my own cousins from Boone County, Emily Todd, were as accomplished as I was. I did have to learn arithmetic, history, geography, natural science, French, and religion. Mrs. Ward taught astronomy and something I liked best. On the afternoons when her husband was busy talking politics in the parlor with professors from Transylvania, she would take us into the kitchen and teach us how to make puddings and custards, cakes and candy.

She also was responsible for having us join the young ladies' library in Lexington and saw to it that we attended performances by every children's theater company as well as performances of Shakespeare and the American premiere of a Beethoven string quartet.

It was impossible not to like Mrs. Ward. Once a month, on a Saturday, she took us shopping and to the confectionery store of Mr. Giron, whose Swiss pastry cook made special meringues and macaroons for us.

I looked up to Mrs. Ward. Until the day she disappointed me.

Every May first the school erected a maypole in the square, and a girl from Fayette County was selected to be crowned Queen of the May.

It was supposed to be the prettiest girl from Fayette County. But Mrs. Ward was overly fond of Bible verses and required that we memorize them. The girl who memorized the most, she promised, would be queen of the May.

"Even if she isn't from Fayette County?" came the question from Emily Todd, my cousin from Boone County, who boarded at the school.

"Yes," Mrs. Ward promised. "It will be a very democratic process. Remember, this is the school where respectability is all. Where discipline hasn't died and emulation doesn't sleep."

I had no desire to be Queen, but my cousin Emily wanted it so badly she swore she'd memorize the most Bible verses.

She enlisted me to listen to her. She memorized 1,373 verses. And before she reached 50, I begged off.

"Do you think I'll get it, Mary? Do you?"

If women ever could run for president of the United States, Emily would be right there in the forefront, I thought.

"She said whoever memorizes the most verses will be crowned," I said quietly.

But it wasn't very democratic.

For one thing, the girls kept reminding Mrs. Ward that the contest had more to do with beauty than Bible verses. "It's supposed to be the prettiest girl," said Virginia Claymont, who came from our county and was the next to prettiest girl in school.

The prettiest was Catherine Drake. But she was from Nicholas County.

"You all get to wear white and march in an elegant parade to James Trotter's grove where a maypole will be erected. We want to make the best display for the school," was the response Mrs. Ward gave us.

Emily recited her verses. Some of us attended the class where a weary Mrs. Ward and her husband, the Reverend, sat and listened approvingly.

One by one, those of us who attended excused ourselves and left.

There was no doubt about it. Emily won, hands down. But Mrs. Ward still wouldn't name her Queen of the May. And we all knew why, especially Emily.

She simply wasn't pretty enough. The school needed a prettier girl. Before the day was over the girls were split and arguing over who should represent the school as Queen.

Mrs. Ward was beside herself. "I can't have this contest turning my girls against each other!" So she turned it into a civics lesson and had us vote for Queen of the May. "Women can't vote," Isabelle Trotter reminded her.

"They can in this school," Mrs. Ward said.

After some very secretive voting and whispering, the votes were counted. I knew most of the girls considered Emily a Miss Prissy-Boots for memorizing all those Bible verses. But the vote, as it turned out, was a tie. It was even, between Catherine Drake and Emily Todd.

"No more of this." Mrs. Ward gathered the little slips of paper with our votes on them and dumped them in a wastepaper basket.

"Catherine Drake will be Queen of the May," she announced.

To the cries of most, that Catherine came from Nicholas County, she paid no heed.

"But you said whoever memorized the most Bible verses," Emily complained.

"That isn't the point. The fighting that has occurred is distasteful to me. Perhaps next year the girls from this county will learn to take this more in stride."

"She turned on us," Emily sobbed to me later in her room where she boarded. "I know I'm not pretty, but does pretty mean everything?"

I hadn't thought so. Until now. It was a distasteful lesson, but perhaps the most important one I was to learn at Ward's, the school where respectability and discipline lived. The school where emulation never slept. And virtue hadn't fled.

"An outsider from Nicholas County has been selected for Queen of the May," the newspaper reported. "Two young ladies held a canopy over her. Their names were Emily Todd from Boone County and Mary Todd from our own Fayette County."

What the newspaper didn't say was that Emily Todd from Boone County had tears in her eyes while she held her part of the canopy.

I WAS NEARLY thirteen years old and my desire for a hoop-skirt hadn't dimmed. Every time I went with Mammy Sally to Cheapside, the marketplace that served Fayette County, and saw the ladies in their hoopskirts, I felt a stab of envy.

To wear a hoopskirt meant you were grown, and I wanted—more than to eat—to be grown like my sisters Elizabeth and Frances.

I didn't envy their lives. They'd had no more than five years of education each. I didn't want to stop learning after only five years. I wanted to go on with my education.

They did nothing but sew and make calls and ride in the barouche with Nelson driving them. And attend lectures, shop, and go to the university to listen to their dance partners' orations. If not that, it was cotillions and late-night suppers where they dined on Maryland oysters, Spanish pickles, and imported herring.

I did envy their slim waists, their bosoms, the way their hoopskirts swung when they walked.

By now Elizabeth was being courted by Ninian Edwards. He was first in his class at Transylvania Law School. His father was governor of Illinois. I considered him a snob, but I had to be nice to him because Elizabeth had told me that after she wed him they would move to Springfield, Illinois, and she would have first Frances come and live with them, and then me. After I had been introduced to Lexington society and taken my place in the social world, of course.

I didn't want to enter the social world just yet, though Elizabeth often reminded me how much my dancing lessons would help, as well as the way I carried myself. And how, being the younger sister of Elizabeth Todd mattered. "I am at the center of the social whirl," she reminded me. "To be a Todd and my younger sister is to carry a full dance card into that whirl when your time comes."

It would soon be necessary to move out of the house as far as I could see. Betsy Todd had had three children in four years and the house on Short Street was getting crowded. The first, Robert, died as a baby.

But before I moved out I wanted that hoopskirt.

FORTUNATELY LIZ HUMPHREYS wanted one as badly as I did. So one day we decided just to make our own hoopskirts, without the help of anyone. I didn't want to drag Grandma into it, because no doubt it would bring trouble down on our heads when Betsy found out, and things weren't so good between her and Grandma Parker as they should have been in the first place.

"First, what will we make them from?" Liz asked. "We don't have any whalebone, and I don't see any whales available around Lexington anyway."

"Willow reeds," I said. "I've been thinking of it a long time. And I know just where to get them."

If, I told myself, Grandmother Jane could make a wedding dress out of weeds and wild flax, why couldn't I make a hoop out of willow reeds? I'd show Betsy Todd what it took to be a true lady. She wouldn't bad-mouth the Todd name when I got through.

Liz and I spent an afternoon at a nearby stream picking the willow reeds. Then we laid them out in the sun to dry. The whole business took time because we were still in school and were pretty much watched when at home, except for an hour or two before dinner when we had free playtime.

I prided myself on always being interested in dressmaking anyway. And so, with Liz watching, I carefully constructed a wide and billowing hoop over which to stretch my good Sunday muslin dresses. Then Liz and I made hers, and we smuggled them up into the house and into the cellar. Betsy never went into the cellar. She was afraid of it. And anyway, she was in a "delicate" condition again, expecting another baby, and so avoided stairs.

On Sunday morning we both put on our good muslin dresses and went down to breakfast. I could scarce eat for excitement, and I saw Liz picking at her food, too. Under the table she kicked me and giggled.

"What's wrong with you two?" Betsy asked. "Behave. It's the Lord's day."

"Behave, Mary," my pa repeated.

Over Pa's head, Mammy Sally looked at me knowingly and shook her head, then continued to pour seconds of coffee around the table.

Finally the meal was finished and we were dismissed to get ready for church. We went to McChord's Presbyterian Church, where most of Lexington's elite went.

Liz and I left the dining room and repaired directly to the cellar, where we struggled into our hoopskirts, then swayed and giggled as we made our way up the stairs and sought out Betsy in the front parlor where she was adjusting Ann's bonnet. She herself would not go to church. She was too near her "time."

The look on her face was worth a thousand words. It was priceless. "What?" she demanded.

"We made our own hoopskirts," I said. "Aren't you proud of us?"

She wasn't.

"What frights you are," she said. "Get those awful things off, dress yourselves properly, and go to church. I'll not have you disgracing the Todd name or your dear father."

Tears choked my throat. I held them back. Liz didn't. She cried openly and loudly.

"This instant," Betsy demanded. "Before I tell your father. Honestly, Mary, I had no idea you would go to such lengths to disgrace and upset me. Go, I said. Before your father sees you."

But it was too late. Pa appeared in the doorway. "What's all the commotion?" He didn't express surprise at the way we looked. He seemed to take it for granted.

I did a little curtsy. "Look at my new hoopskirt, Pa."

Well, he couldn't see the hoop, of course. All he could see was the muslin dress all puffed out. "You look nice, both of you," he said. "Now what's going on? Mary, are you upsetting Betsy again?"

"She isn't supposed to be wearing a hoopskirt," Betsy told him firmly. "She is too young and she knows it. I didn't buy it for her. She made it. And Liz's."

"Made it?" He seemed surprised.

"Yes, Pa. Like Grandmother Jane made her wedding dress. Grandma told me all about that."

He lowered his gaze. Was he smiling? Was he proud of me? Dare he tell Betsy?

"If your mother told you you can't have one, then you disobeyed her," he said. "And so you'll have to stay away from Grandma Parker for the next month."

"Pa!" I wailed.

Now he scowled. "No mouth," he ordered. "Now go take it off."

We went. Betsy personally destroyed our hoopskirts and burned the willow reeds. But I know that I could be like Grandmother Jane if I had to be. And I know Pa was proud of me.

It was in my last year at Ward's that I awoke one night in November to hear *thump thump thump*ing coming from downstairs, likely the back door in the kitchen. As I lay warm and snuggly under my quilts, I then heard Mammy Sally shuffling around. Then the thumping stopped.

Liz heard it, too. "What's that noise, Mary?"

"I don't know." I sat up. "But I'm going to see."

"No, don't go. Maybe it's Indians attacking. Don't leave me, Mary." She was sleeping with her Pierre huddled next to her. Unfortunately, Pierre heard the thumping, too, because he sat up and woofed. Short little woofs, the kind he might give in a dream. I hushed him and patted his head and he settled down again. And when I saw that he had quieted, I put on my robe and crept downstairs, assuring Liz it wasn't Indians.

"They'd come to the front door," I told her.

As I peeked into the kitchen, I saw a candle lit, casting a peculiar light across the floor. I stood there trembling as Mammy opened the back door.

What huddled there could scarce be called a man. He was kneeling down, wrapped in rags, and looking up at Mammy appealingly. "You put the sign on the back fence, auntie?"

"My name is Mammy Sally. I ain't nobody's auntie. But yes, I put the sign on the fence. I'll feed you and clothe you and get you on your way to the Ohio River. But you can't stay the night. Master'll sell me down the river fer sure, he finds out I'm doin' this."

"Grateful, Mammy, grateful," the man said.

"Now you go on back to the barn. I'll bring out some victuals. Meat an' bread and somethin' warm fer you to wear," she told him.

Then she closed the door in his face and turned. And saw me.

"What you doin' there, chil'?" the harsh whisper came across the kitchen.

"I heard the thumping."

"Well you best forget what you hear, or you'll be hearin' Mammy wail at bein' sold downriver."

"Can I go outside with you to bring his food?"

"No. An' you ain't to go tellin' anybody else 'bout this. If your stepma finds out, I'll be horse fodder.

"Now go to bed," she directed. And I promised I would, as I watched her gather food in the kitchen. Then we both heard the stairs creak behind us in the hall and froze.

It was Liz.

"What you doin' here?" Mammy Sally said in a loud whisper. "What is this, a May Day parade?"

"I wanted to see," Liz stammered.

"See what?" Mammy asked.

"I don't know. I was afraid it was Indians come to scalp us."

"Only me," Mammy told her, "an' I'll scalp you if'n you doan get up to bed now."

Liz turned and ran. I stayed to watch Mammy Sally go out the back door to the barn with a single lantern in tow along with some victuals.

The next day I asked her, "How do they know to come to our house?"

She chuckled. "You invited them."

"Me?"

"Yes. 'Member the day you painted those flowers on the front of the fence?"

"You helped me, Mammy."

"Yes, but you didn't know why you were doin' it, did you?"

"I thought I was just painting some flowers on the fence."

"No. You were invitin' runaways to stop. You were tellin' 'em that here, in this place, if they wuz careful they could get food and clothes on their way to crossin' the Ohio River."

"You mean we're part of the Underground Railroad?"

"No," she shook her head vigorously. "We ain't. I just helps 'em move along. An's you better talk to that Liz girl. If'n she tells her aunt Betsy, we're all finished."

I just stared at her in wonderment. I was young enough to think it all exciting and to think of Mammy Sally as a negro Joan of Arc. To think, right in the midst of us all, this was going on. But I had a question.

"How long have you been doing this?" I asked.

"Not long 'nuf."

I continued staring while she kneaded some pie dough.

"Things ain't always what you think, little one," she told me. And then she chuckled. "The next time you paint some flowers on a fence, think what you might be really doin'."

"It was just a traveler who lost his way last night," I told Liz later that morning.

We were both knitting. It was Saturday. And I wondered if my "traveler" had gotten safely to the Ohio River.

"I'm not stupid, Mary. I know what it was. I know Mammy Sally is using this place as a safe house for runaways."

I was trembling inside. Would she hold this over me now? Make me do things I didn't want to do? She had every chance to lord it over me, and there wasn't a thing I could do about it.

"I looked out our upstairs window and saw her taking the food to the barn," she said. "What else could it be? We have people who do it in Frankfort, too."

"Liz, if you tell your aunt Betsy . . . ," I started to say.

She leveled her blue eyes at me. "I said I'm not stupid," she repeated.

"But your people believe in slavery."

She shrugged. "Didn't they tell us at Ward's to think for ourselves?"

I breathed a sigh of relief.

"And Mary, I won't hold this over you. You don't have to worry. If you don't really trust me yet, I want you to know that."

Like Mammy Sally said, things ain't always what they seem to be. And the next time I went to paint flowers on a fence I'd remember that.

WHEN I WAS THIRTEEN, I got my pony.

At breakfast Pa said he had something to show me outside. I should have known what it was because of the looks and giggles of everyone at the table. And because of what Betsy said.

"Robert, you didn't."

"Yes I did, Betsy. Though it was forced on me. Payment for a debt I was owed. I thought, why not?"

"Because she's a little ruffian now. She needs no more encouragement."

He murmured something back to her. I couldn't hear what. Because by now Nelson was leading over to me the most beautiful cream-colored pony I had ever seen.

"Mary, this is Peaches," Pa said. "He's yours."

"Providing you behave yourself," Betsy put in. "Or I'll take away riding privileges."

"He's yours," Pa said again.

I embraced the little darling, who put his nose into my shoulder just as if he knew he belonged to me. I patted him, happier than I'd been in a long time. "Can I take him for a ride?" I asked. There was a regular saddle on him.

"Only sidesaddle," Betsy directed. "Like a lady."

"Go ahead," Pa said. And he helped me astride Peaches.

"I think I'll go to Mr. Clay's house and show him. He's been asking me when I'm going to get my pony."

My family waved me off. Senator Henry Clay lived a mile and a half outside town. His home was called Ashland. He came out on the front portico holding a dinner napkin, when I was announced.

"Well, and hello to you, my pretty little Miss Todd. What do we have here?"

"The new pony Pa gave me for my birthday. His name is Peaches."

He came off the portico to help me down and to pat Peaches. "A fine specimen of pony. But you deserve him. Will you come in and dine with us? I have a guest. John Crittenden. You know him."

"Are you talking politics?"

"Always. Are you still supporting me in my presidential aspirations?"

"Always."

I left my pony on the limestone gravel drive with the senator's negro, Sanborn, and went into the gracious house.

They did discuss politics at dinner and I did listen. Senator Clay was about to leave for Washington City, and he asked me if there was anything of importance I wanted him to see to.

I thought for a moment. "All the things I want can't be given by Congress, Mr. Clay," I told him.

"And if I could give them to you, I would."

"You could let me visit with you when you live in the White House."

"Dear girl, I don't know whether that will ever come to be. But as far as I'm concerned you have a room there."

With such a promise intact and my pony waiting outside, I had one of the few happy days that I remember during that time.

By early 1832 there were nine Todd children in the house, to Betsy's dismay. From my sister Elizabeth, who was nineteen, down to one-year-old Samuel, Betsy's third child.

And she was again in a delicate condition, expecting her fourth.

Her patience was tried. She cried most of the time. She took to her room and stayed there and left the doings of the household to the servants.

Then came the announcement from my sister Elizabeth that she was to marry Ninian Edwards and move to Springfield, Illinois. When they had settled she would invite Frances to live with them.

I think it was the only thing that kept Betsy sane. And I think she wished that Elizabeth would also take me. I know I did.

Elizabeth's wedding took place in the house and the whole place was in an uproar for two weeks preceding. Liz and I were invited to be bridesmaids, and here is where I got my say in a matter of grave importance to me.

"If I'm to be a bridesmaid, I should have a hoop," I told Betsy. "Liz, too. How would it look for others to wear hoops and not us?"

"You're still too young," was her reply.

"If I can't have a hoop, I don't want to be a bridesmaid. And I'm too old to scatter rose petals. So that means I can't be in my sister's wedding. And I know Pa wants me to be in the wedding."

"You are a limb of Satan," she said, "to corner me so."

"If I could go to Springfield with Elizabeth, I would."

"You're too young. But you are going somewhere. You and Liz are going to Madame Mentelle's Boarding School when you graduate from Ward's. Your education isn't finished."

"I don't want it to be."

She was doing some embroidery. And never once did she look up at me. "What you don't know is that you will stay there all week, and Nelson will fetch Liz home every evening. That is what you don't know."

I felt the room swirl in front of me. Something fell and crashed on the floor of my soul. She was putting me out. As discreetly as she could.

I had won my hoopskirt, but at what price? Like Mammy Sally had said, the next time I painted flowers on a fence I should stop and think about what I was really doing.

WE HAD A CRISIS in our house before my sister Elizabeth's wedding.

Grandma Parker said she would not come.

"I haven't been down there since your father married that woman," she told us. "I can't come now."

To my surprise it was me Pa asked to influence her to come down. He called me into his study one day and I went, sure I had done something wrong, but unable to think what.

Either that or he was going to tell me about my boarding at Mentelle's, a fact we hadn't discussed yet. I had consoled myself by thinking that if Pa hadn't yet mentioned it to me, it wasn't so. And by that same token, I wouldn't mention it to him.

"Mary, dear child," he said as I entered his study. "How are you keeping these days?"

My pa could be charming. And as much as you knew he was using his charm on you, it didn't make any difference. You couldn't resist it.

"I'm fine, Pa," I said.

"And how is that pony of yours?"

"Peaches is very frisky."

"Have you shown him to Grandmother Parker yet?"

"No."

"That's what I wanted to ask you to do for me, Mary. Take a ride up the hill and show him to Grandmother Parker."

He wanted more than that. I knew it, and he knew that I knew it. "Don't make me be the one to ask her to come to the wedding, Pa."

He leaned forward on his desk. "She loves you best. She'll do it for you. How do you think it looks with my eldest daughter getting married and her grandmother not being at the wedding? How will it look to the guests?"

"Like she doesn't want to come," I said flippantly.

He scowled. "Don't be sassy, Mary. I'm in a fix here. A real fix. I depend on you to get me out of it. You have the gift of talking anybody into anything."

He was appealing to me. And he was my pa, my dear pa. How could I say no? I said yes, sorry the minute I had said it.

GRANDMOTHER PARKER was rolling out pie dough, but she wiped her hands and came right outside to see Peaches. "You ride astride, I see," she commented.

"Yes. No sidesaddle for me, Grandma."

"I don't blame you. I always wanted to ride like that. Good luck with the pony, child. Now come inside and have some fresh-baked cookies and tell me what you really came for. As if I don't know."

In her warm, cheerful kitchen she placed before me fresh-baked sugar cookies, some slices of ham, and cold milk.

"It's the wedding, isn't it? They've chosen you to soften me up."

What could I say? I admired her so, her spunk, her determination, her single-mindedness. How could I ask her to go against her principles?

"Grandma, Pa wants you to come in the worst way. So does Elizabeth. She says it won't be a family wedding without you. She says you are the matriarch and the guests would be disappointed not to see you."

She chewed this over in her mind. "I hate that Betsy," she said.

"I know, Grandma. We all do. But we have to live with her."

"You poor child. I'd have you here in a minute if your father would allow it."

"Just come on this important day, Grandma, and take Ma's place."

Her eyes watered. "What will Betsy be wearing?"

"Something in powder blue with ruffles and lace."

"I have my lavender. I only wear it on very special occasions."

"Oh, Grandma, you look like a queen in it!"

"I don't want to look like a queen. If I come, I just want to look like a grandmother who should be reckoned with."

My heart beat fast. "Will you come then?"

"I said *if.*"

I waited. You didn't push with Grandmother, and I'd already pushed far enough. I didn't want to paint any more flowers on fences without knowing what I was inviting in.

"If I come, I speak my mind," she said. "I won't be shackled."

"Everyone loves you, Grandma. We know you'll make us proud."

I left without knowing if she were coming or not. She was not without a sense of drama, my grandmother. If she came, she wanted it to be a surprise. She wanted everyone to wonder.

That's what I told Pa. It was all I could tell him. He only smiled and patted my head. "You make a fine go-between, Mary," he said. "Too bad you aren't a boy. You could be an excellent politician. Someday perhaps you'll make use of your talents."

A boy, I thought. *Yes, I'd like to be a boy. I'd run for president.*

THE DAY OF ELIZABETH's wedding was sky-blue clear, as fine a day as mid-February could offer. Just about spring in Lexington, Kentucky.

Early in the morning Liz and I went into the room Elizabeth shared with Frances. Mammy Sally had brought up coffee and sweet buns, and as if we'd planned it, we girls sprawled around and had a party, paying homage to Elizabeth's last day at home. Liz was to be in the wedding party, too. As were Ann and Frances and little Margaret. Margaret, just four years old, was my half sister.

Elizabeth's wedding dress hung in the corner. It had been Mama's, and we looked at it in silent admiration, each thinking our own thoughts.

"I wish she were here." Elizabeth's voice had a catch in it.

"She is," Frances said.

Elizabeth had tears in her eyes. "Is Grandmother Parker coming?" she asked me.

"Yes," I lied. "She'll be here. She won't let you down. Don't worry."

We all were going to dress for the wedding together in Elizabeth's room. All around, on the bed and chairs and dripping out of the highboy, were her traveling clothes. Mammy climbed the stairs with her lumbering gait and came into the room to start packing.

"You want I should help you into your weddin' dress?" she said.

"Yes, in a minute," Elizabeth said. She was wiping some tears from her eyes.

Mammy stood before it, touched it lightly. "I 'members the day I helped your own mama into it," she said. "My, she was right pretty. An' I 'spect you'll be just as pretty, Miz Elizabeth."

"Thank you," Elizabeth said. She brushed some crumbs from her morning robe. There was a moment's silence, and then someone stood in the doorway.

Betsy. She stood staring at Elizabeth for a long moment. "You'd best dress," she said. "The guests are starting to arrive."

"Yes," Elizabeth said.

"That grandmother of yours has not yet shown her face. You'd think, if she was coming, she'd be here by now," she said.

"She'll be here," I said firmly.

Betsy looked at me. "We'll see how good your powers of persuasion are. Your father thinks you are so wonderful. Well let me tell you," and she switched her attention to Elizabeth again. "This isn't your day. It's mine. It's mine because I kept this family together after your mother died. I did my duty by you all."

Grandmother, please come, I prayed. *Please come. We need you.*

ELIZABETH WOULD PASS under an arch made of forsythia blossoms in the parlor to stand before Reverend Davidson from McChord's Presbyterian.

I dressed in the pink organdy especially made by Betsy's dressmaker. Pa had brought back yards and yards of it for me and Frances, Liz, Ann, and Margaret.

Actually it had been a present for me. Every time I had a fight with Betsy, I knew Pa wasn't going to take my side. I didn't expect him to. He might even scold me, but he would always give me presents. Kid gloves or yards and yards of yellow muslin or the latest in bonnets.

In the kitchen Mammy was now presiding over the food. In the back parlor Ninian Edwards stood with his friends from Transylvania, talking of plays and what horses they wanted to bet on and drinking strong black coffee topped with whipped cream and shaved chocolate. Ninian looked as if he came from the most socially and politically prominent family in Illinois. His father, who was governor of that state, could not come today.

I peeked into the dining room. The table was open as long as it could go and covered with the whitest of damask cloths. A dozen or more candles in silver candelabra waited to be lighted. Silverware gleamed. Soon the table would be laden with preserved meats from France, turkey and cured ham, mounds of mashed potatoes, green vegetables, iced melon, chocolate-covered strawberries, the softest of Mammy Sally's biscuits, and later the lightest of wedding cakes, covered with filmy whipped icing from Giron's Confectioners.

At the front door Nelson stood with Betsy and Pa, greeting guests. Soon most everyone was seated in chairs in the front parlor, talking in whispers and waiting to see the bride.

Everyone but Grandmother Parker.

"Go upstairs and get your sisters," Betsy rushed by me and whispered.

But I couldn't move. My eyes were glued to Nelson and Pa, still waiting at the front door. And past him to the front drive where any minute, I knew, Grandmother's carriage would pull up.

I heard it before I saw it. Heard the wheels on the limestone drive, the snorting of the horses, the rattling of the harnesses. She was here!

Everyone else sensed it, too. In the front parlor people craned their necks to look out the windows. Some got up and went to the windows.

"Look at that," one elderly man said. "She looks as imperious as the day she rode into town from Pennsylvania as the bride of Major Robert Parker."

Everyone agreed. I went out the front door to greet her. She was wearing her lavender with the high neck and long sleeves, and she was as straight and as lovely as a bride herself. I was afraid to hug her, afraid to muss her dress, but she enveloped me in her arms.

"Grandmother, you came."

"Of course I did. Did you expect me not to? Where are my girls?"

She came in the hall asking the question, "Where are my girls?"

"Grandmother Parker, we're ready to start," Betsy said, standing in front of her.

"Not until I see my girls in private."

Ninian and his friends came out of the back parlor then at the sound of her voice. They each, in turn, took her hand and kissed it. Then I led her up the stairs to Elizabeth's room. Looking down from the top of the stairs, I could see Betsy standing there, hands on her hips, looking angry as a fox in a leg trap.

ELIZABETH AND NINIAN LEFT. It was an eight- or nine-day trip to Springfield, depending on the weather. Ninian was to be a member of the Illinois legislature. His father was the richest man in Springfield, and he and Elizabeth were to occupy the largest house. Oh how I envied Frances, going to live with them in a couple of months.

Springfield is still the frontier. Yet, Elizabeth told me, they have a society all their own. They adhere to all the social rules. And it is a town that attracts politicians. I would so dearly love to go.

But I'm not finished with my schooling. And after Elizabeth left, Pa finally came out and told me, yes, I was to board at Mentelle's during the week.

"Liz, too?" I asked.

We were in his study. "No. She is to come home each day." He did not look at me.

"Then I'm being put out of my own home."

"No, Mary. You will always belong here. I just feel it's better this way."

"You mean Betsy does."

"Mary, you'll be a mile and a half from home. Many girls your age go to boarding school. It is really Liz who is the loser. Betsy doesn't think she is mature enough for the experience. You should be flattered that she thinks you are. The experience alone will add to your personality, your list of achievements, and your social graces. Right now some fine young man whom you will someday marry is away at boarding school getting the best preparation for life. Does my daughter deserve any less?"

My father's charm would be the death of me yet, I decided. He could persuade a savage Indian to take tea in the parlor.

I missed Elizabeth when she left. Sometimes, as an older sister, she plagued me. She was so perfect, so pretty, so correct about everything. But since Mama had died, when she was eleven, she had always looked after us younger ones, and almost replaced Mama in many ways. The house, for all its people, was empty without her.

There was one less at the table. Which brought Pa to his next problem. So again he called me into his study.

"Mary, you've got to help me do something about George."

Why now? I thought. *This last year you haven't cared about George.*

My brother, George Rogers Clark, ate all his meals in the kitchen, alone at the table this past year.

It was an embarrassment to the family and a decision of his own choosing. George, of his own accord, removed himself from most family gatherings and activities to the extent that Pa would let him get away with it.

Eating at the table with the family was one activity he'd refused to take part in.

It was all really very simple. George blamed himself for Ma's death, for tearing the family apart. And if he was made to sit at the table with us, he wouldn't eat.

So Pa let him get away with his self-imposed punishment. Guests soon became accustomed to it, considered George a little "odd" at best.

Now Pa decided he wanted George back at the family table. And he was going to ask me to approach my seven-year-old rebellious brother, like he'd asked me to approach Grandmother Parker about the wedding.

"Pa, there's nothing to be done about George. Except one thing."

"What's that?"

"If Betsy would ask him to come to the table, I think he'd come."

He scowled. "You can't expect me to ask Betsy to beg a seven-year-old to eat with us, if he doesn't want to."

Why not? I thought. *She's supposed to be the mother around here.*

"George is becoming more and more odd as time goes by," he said. "He just about talks only to his tutor. The only boy he'll play with is his brother Levi. I can't let him grow up like this, Mary. So I'm asking you to talk to him. I've already had all the doctors who attended your mother that day talk to him and tell him it wasn't his fault. Tell him now that I'll get Harriet Leuba, the watchmaker's wife, to come and talk to him, too."

Harriet Leuba was the most famous of the midwives in Fayette County, and she'd been attending Ma in the birth before the doctors were called in.

"All right, Pa," I said. "I'll try."

"Good girl."

That night at the supper table Pa signaled to me with a gesture of his head. I had noticed a place setting where Elizabeth used to sit, so I got up, excused myself, and went into the kitchen. There Mammy Sally was icing a cake for dessert. And George sat quietly sipping some soup.

He was big for seven, all hands and feet, with reddish blond, curly hair, freckles, and alert blue eyes. *How proud Mama would have been of him,* I thought. I sat down opposite him.

"George, how is the soup?" I asked.

"Mammy Sally never made better."

She chuckled from a table in the corner.

I got right at it. "Pa wants you to come and eat with us at the table, George," I said.

He continued sipping his soup. "Pa knows I can't do that."

"Why?"

"I already told him."

"Tell me, then."

He put down his spoon and looked at me. "I can't belong to this family anymore. I tore it apart. You think I don't see how torn apart it is? How you and the others hate Betsy?"

"It isn't your fault, George. Three doctors already told you that."

"I'd like to know whose fault it is then, if not mine. I killed her. I killed Ma. Nobody else."

"You didn't. She died of the fever. And Pa says he'll get Harriet Leuba, the midwife, to come in and tell you if you want."

"I don't want. Pa wants it. Look, Mary, you have your own troubles. Leave me alone."

"We miss you, George. We miss you at the table and at other things. Where did you go to at the wedding? We missed you then."

"I had things to do." He didn't look at me. Then he cast an eye at Mammy, who was still icing and humming softly. Then he whispered to me, "Anyways, you-all ought to be watching Levi instead of me."

"Why?" I asked.

He shrugged and looked at Mammy again. Then more whispering. "You know those times when he says he's fishing at the creek?"

"Yes."

"Well, he may be fishing, but he's drinking, too."

A stab of fear went through me. Levi was almost fifteen, a year older than I was. My mouth fell open.

"Don't go telling anybody now," George said.

"No," I promised. "I won't." And I stood up, rather shaky in my legs. What else was going on in this house that Pa and Betsy didn't know about. Levi drinking! Where was he getting the liquor? Well, that was easy enough. Out of Pa's study. Oh, what had happened to my family since Ma died? George knew. George saw, though only seven. And he blamed it all on himself and was punishing himself for it.

"You won't come and join us then?" I asked.

He only gave a short laugh and waved me away.

George was a grown man, I decided as I left the kitchen. If only Pa knew the all of it.

LATE THAT NIGHT when everybody was in bed, I heard Mammy moving about in the kitchen, so I got up and went downstairs.

She was churning butter. A fresh loaf of bread lay on the table in front of her.

She smiled at me as I approached. "You heard?" I asked.

"Yes, child, I heard. Old Mammy got ears like the debil, though they ain't been painted green."

"I don't know whether to worry about George or Levi first," I told her.

"Worry 'bout yourself. You gots enough to worry 'bout. You goin' away to school in the fall and then there's movin'."

"Moving? Who's moving?"

"They ain't told you?"

"No."

"Your daddy been biddin' for Palmentier's Inn. It for sale."

How Mammy Sally knew everything that went on in

the family before I did was a matter of mystery to me. Maybe because she did have ears like the debil. At any rate I had no trouble attributing special powers to her. Black people did have special powers, I'd long since decided. They must have, to put up with what they had to bear. Besides, those like Mammy had to continually move between two worlds.

But moving! Moving out of the house where I'd been brought up, where Mama had lived? And died? I suspected George and Levi wouldn't think much of the house on Main Street even if it was grander than this.

And then another thought came to me.

"What about the runaways?" I asked Mammy.

She shook her head. "I just hafta pass the word on that they shud come to the new house. It got a barn an' a fence around it. You wanna paint some flowers on that fence when the time comes?"

I took a deep breath. "Yes."

"Good."

"Mammy, what would I do without you?"

"You'd be jus' fine. You're quality, Mary. You'd be jus' fine."

"I don't ever want to leave you." I stifled a sob.

"You gots to leave sometime. You find yourself another mammy somewhere along the way."

"Is there anything you can do for George and Levi?"

"I kin' talk to 'em. Not sayin' they'll listen."

I hugged her. She gave me a piece of fresh bread and butter before I went to bed.

Levi was to go to Transylvania in the fall. At first he refused, angering Pa, and they had high words, but then Mammy Sally got ahold of him and they "talked." I think she threatened to tell Pa about his drinking down by the creek. And so he agreed to go and to behave himself. Already, as summer came upon us, he was registered and had his books. He was to attend day classes and come home each night.

Ann was to go to Ward's and, of course, come home at night. I found myself envying her. I wanted to go back to my first year at Ward's when I had such innocence. I was afraid of Mentelle's, afraid of what was expected of me. Pa expected a lot.

Pa had ideas about the education of girls. Somehow Elizabeth and Frances had escaped the full range of those ideas, being brought up mainly by Ma. But now, since my mother's death or maybe because of it, Pa was determined that the rest of his girls have the best education possible. And not leave school at thirteen, as Frances and Elizabeth had done, to become accomplished at nothing but dancing and social graces.

I registered for school with Liz. We walked together up to Rose Hill, the name of the building the school was housed in. It was a sprawling, rambling gabled place with different wings jutting out unexpectedly and white organdy curtains at all the windows.

"I heard there are about twenty motherless girls here," Liz told me as we trudged up the hill.

"I guess I'm number twenty-one then."

"Mary, don't hold it against me that I'm going home every night and you're not."

"I'm not holding it against you."

"Yes you are. You've been acting different lately. Not friendly anymore."

"I've got a lot to think about."

"What?"

I couldn't tell her my concerns about George and Levi. My sadness at moving. She wouldn't understand. "It isn't you, Liz, I promise," I said.

"I feel as if I've taken your place."

"I have no place. So don't worry about it. There're eight of us home now. David is only three months old and Betsy needs more room for her babies. So she gets a new house and me out of it most of the time."

"Your pa loves you, Mary. I know he does."

"He can afford to love me only so much. Then he has to do what she wants. And she wants me out."

"She's my very own aunt, but I'm ashamed of the way she treats you sometimes," Liz said.

"There's only one thing I want," I told her. "I want my ma's ladies' desk. Pa said once that I could have it. And I aim to take it when they move. I know a lot of things will be sold because she wants all new things. Fancy red damask drapes and Belgian carpets and imported French mahogany furniture. But I want that desk for my own."

"You'll have it," Liz promised.

But I worried. It wasn't her place to say so.

"Welcome to Mentelle's School for Young Ladies," Charlotte Mentelle greeted us.

She was a small, lively woman, with bright blue eyes and a little knot of hair atop her head, tied with a black velvet ribbon. "Sit down, girls, sit. Did you know we are across the way from Senator Henry Clay's Ashland?"

We said yes.

"And did you know one of my daughters is married to Henry Clay's son, Thomas?"

She puffed with pride. Yes, we said, we knew that, too.

"Well, and so you are going to be part of my school. This is a proud school and we uphold standards. You will be learning French, morals, temper, and health, among other things. I give no holidays but one week at Christmas, one day for Easter, and one day for Whitsuntide. You will act in French plays and dance while I play the fiddle. Mary Todd, do you realize what a wonderful father you have?"

"Yes, ma'am," I said meekly. One did not oppose this woman. I could see that immediately.

She wore a white dress this summer's day. We were to discover that she wore white all summer long and blue all winter, that, like her husband, she was an expert fiddle player, that she loved to terrorize the girls with stories of her childhood when they misbehaved, and that she had six children of her own, three still at home.

She made a big fuss over Liz, sending her into the parlor to have tea while she took me to see my room. She liked Liz's blond curls and Bo-Peep look. Everybody did.

As for me, I liked the look of her house. It looked comfortable and lived-in, with plumped pillows on all the couches, books in every room, heart pine floors, and woven rugs. An English springer spaniel accompanied us through the house, licking my hand as we went.

"The dog helps girls to feel at home," she told me. "Ah, here, this will be your room. You will share with a lovely girl named Mercy Levering."

Sunlight streamed in the windows. The beds had quilts covering them. There were flowers in a vase on a dresser. And then I had a thought.

"Is there room for a small desk?" I asked Mrs. Mentelle.

"I usually don't allow the girls to bring furniture."

"It was my mother's," I explained. "And with my family planning on moving, I'm afraid it will get lost."

"Well then, we'll make room," she agreed, "if it was your mother's. Everybody knows how important things are when they come from your mother."

I think I loved her on the spot.

JUST ABOUT EVERY summer my family traveled fifty miles south to Crab Orchard Springs where we could take the waters, play, and socialize with other prominent families in the area.

That summer we didn't go. That summer was different and the worst I ever remember.

That summer cholera came to Lexington.

First came the rain, a pouring rain, for days, that made the privies overflow and the streams contaminated. There was a dreadful smell in the air everywhere, even after the rains stopped. The newspapers warned people not to drink water from the streams. Pa forbade Levi and George to go near Elkhorn Creek behind our house.

Then one day Mrs. Holmdel, who lived on Water Street, became ill. Her mammy met Mammy Sally at the market and told Mammy Sally that her mistress had all the signs of cholera. By nightfall Mrs. Holmdel was dead. Word went around from house to house. People knew what the disease was because it had already killed thousands in New York City and New Orleans. Last summer, Pa's sister, Aunt Hannah, had died from it when it visited outlying parts of Kentucky.

Now it was here.

By the end of the first week, ten people were dead of it.

The rest kept their doors and shutters locked, their children inside, and their businesses closed. The town was empty except for the dead carts rattling through to pick up bodies.

"We must leave," Betsy told Pa. "We endanger the children by staying. We should go to Buena Vista." It was her country estate on the Leestown Pike near Frankfort.

"Cholera is in the countryside, too," Pa told her, "and as a city councilman, I must stay. You may take the little ones and the baby and go if you wish, Betsy. I'll send George and Levi with you, and Nelson can drive you to the country."

She decided to stay.

We burned tar in barrels to stave off the disease. Mammy Sally had the other servants wash down the walls with vinegar and spread so much lime about the outside of the house you nearly choked for the smell of it. We were allowed to eat only biscuits, eggs, boiled milk, and water.

One day I ate some mulberries. They were sitting there on the sink in the kitchen and I thought, *What harm can they do?* So I ate them.

Betsy and Mammy found out at the same time and you never did hear such screaming and carrying on. Betsy sent for the doctor. Before he could come Mammy Sally got the ipecac and held my nose as I fought her.

"If the doctor come, he give you mercury chloride," Mammy scolded. "He bleed you. You want that?"

I didn't, so I took the ipecac and threw up. The boys laughed and enjoyed the whole thing. The new baby, David, cried. Pa was furious.

"There are people dying all around us, and you-all are making a mockery of this," he scolded. Pa never scolded, so we quieted down.

In the terrible, ghostly days that followed, we tried to stay out of one another's way, for the crowding in the house. When Levi and George couldn't abide it any longer they sneaked outside to look up and down Short Street, where the living were throwing the dead people out the windows to be picked up by the dead carts that came around for the bodies.

"They're blue," I heard Levi tell George, who was always hungry for otherworldly information. "Their hands and feet are all puckered. Their tongues are hanging out."

I caught them often in whispered conversation and knew they were discussing the victims. Doctor Joseph Boswell had succumbed to the dreadful disease. So had Captain Postlewaite and Mrs. Charles Wickcliffe. I don't know where they got their information from, but they had their ungodly contacts. Besides, though Pa would not let any of us out of the house, he allowed them to go out for an hour every day to check up on Grandma Parker, to see if she was keeping and if she needed anything. I wanted to go, of course, but he wouldn't let me.

And then one evening at supper I looked up from

pushing my eggs around on my plate to see them looking at me oddly.

"Why are you looking at me like that?" I asked, only to realize that others at the table would not even meet my gaze. I shivered.

"Is Grandma all right?"

"She's fine," Pa answered, "but, Mary dear, two of your school chums from Mrs. Ward's have died."

I felt such relief that Grandma was all right that I scarce heard him. Then I did hear. "Who?"

"Emily Houston and Charlotte Wallace."

"Oh." I stared down at my eggs and biscuits. Emily and Charlotte. We hadn't been close, but still, now they were dead! What had it been like for them? Had they been frightened? I shuddered and it came to me then. Any of us could die. I could die, too.

I started to cry and got up and went to Pa, who took me on his lap. And nobody, especially not Levi or George, laughed at me. As a matter of fact, they looked most serious.

There came a pounding on our front door then, and Nelson went to answer it. We heard him saying, "Ain't nobody dead here."

Pa set me down and went into the hallway. I was right behind him. So were Levi and George and Ann.

It was Old Sol, the town gravedigger. He was short and squat. Behind him in our drive was his donkey harnessed to his dead cart. "I needs to see Mr. Todd," he said.

"What is it?" Pa asked.

"Sir, I'm outa coffins. I got no more. So I'm askin' at all

the houses if the people will go to their attics and find what boxes and chests they got and donate 'em."

"Fine. We'll do that," Pa said.

"I'm runnin' outa space in the church cemeteries. Gonna have to start usin' that trench in the new graveyard on the corner of Main and Limestone."

Main and Limestone! A block from our new house. Levi nudged me.

"You do what you have to do," Pa told him. "I'll have some chests out here for you tomorrow."

They closed the door and Pa turned to us. "It'll give you children something to do tomorrow," he said. "Go to the attic, select the biggest chests, and empty them. Nelson will bring them down to put out front."

We nodded, saying nothing. We were stunned, I think, for since Ma died we were never allowed in the attic. In the attic were her things, and Pa and Betsy didn't want us up there, poring over them and getting all cast down.

Now he was allowing us up there.

"Is that wise?" Betsy asked from the background.

"We're moving soon," Pa told her. "All those things have got to be gone through sooner or later."

THE NEXT MORNING after breakfast Levi, Ann, and I made ready to go to the attic. Halfway up the stairs Levi turned to George who stood at the bottom.

"You coming?" he asked.

I saw the indecision on George's face. "Pa said I don't have to if I don't want."

"Come on." Levi extended his hand. "You and I'll go through Pa's things. All that stuff from the war. Let the girls do the rest."

So we four went to the attic. I was trembling with anticipation. How much of Ma's things had Pa saved? And why hadn't he allowed Betsy to convince him to throw them away?

The boys weren't interested in Ma's things. There was a lot of Pa's old stuff to be gone through from the war back in 1812. One chest was labeled LEXINGTON LIGHT ARTILLERY, and Levi and George couldn't wait to get their hands on it.

"You shouldn't be handling those knives and haversacks and guns." Ann was starting to sound more and more like Betsy every day.

As for me, I was already starting to open a chest of Ma's things.

"If it isn't big enough to hold a body, don't bother with it," Levi said with his wicked sense of humor.

I raised the lid of the chest and gasped. Here was everything I imagined as it would be. There were petticoats, silk dresses, shawls, even embroidered aprons. I touched each article reverently.

"Come on, get it out. We don't have all day. You know Pa wants Nelson to bring the chests downstairs by this afternoon," Ann said.

"These are Ma's things, Ann," I told her. Across the attic I saw George looking at me as I raised a tea-colored blouse in the air.

She shrugged. "I know."

"Don't you want to go through them? And see what you'd like to keep?"

She shook her head. "It won't bring her back. Come on, I'll help you stack them in a corner someplace."

I put the blouse down. George went back to Pa's things.

Ann and I had never been close. She was closer to Frances, who spent all her time going to lectures at Transylvania and teas, and sewing things for when it was her time to go to Springfield. Was Ann hiding her true feelings for Ma? Or did she truly not care?

We found an old blanket and wrapped Ma's clothes in them. "I'm going to ask for that shawl," I said, pointing to a black silk one.

"Don't bother," Ann said. "I heard Betsy say everything up here was going out to the first gypsies who came through."

I made a note to ask Pa for what I wanted. Not now, though, not today, not with people throwing dead bodies out their windows and Old Sol collecting boxes and chests for coffins. Pa was a city councilman. He would be busy.

By the end of summer the cholera was past and we who were boarding at Mentelle's were allowed to move our things into our rooms. Pa sent Nelson to accompany me with my baggage and Mama's gold and white ladies' desk in the wagon. Nelson was to carry everything upstairs.

The moving took near all day, and when I got home, the first thing I did was go up to the attic to get the clothes from Ma that Pa said I could have.

They would be kept at Grandma Parker's. She had agreed to it.

I went across the attic room to open the blanket. The clothes were not there! They were gone.

I stood stunned for a minute, thinking. Where had they gone? Had Nelson brought them to Grandma Parker's? I held the empty blanket in my hand, wondering.

Had Ann or Frances become interested in them after all?

And then I was struck with fear. Betsy! And I knew where the clothing had disappeared to.

I went downstairs on shaky legs. I heard her in the kitchen, talking to Mammy Sally about supper.

She saw me standing in the doorway. "So, you're home. How did the moving go? Did you get your room in order?"

I had the empty blanket in my hands. She saw it but said nothing.

"Where is my mama's clothing that was in the corner of the attic in this blanket?" I asked.

"Heavens, Mary, you wanted that old stuff?"

"Where is it?"

"Some strolling players came through today. I gave it to them."

"You gave away my mama's blue taffeta dress? Her lace collars? Her black fringed shawl from New Orleans?"

"Well, it was all old and moth-eaten. What could you possibly want with it?"

"That was for me to decide!" I was crying. Tears were coming down my face. "Pa said I could have it. Nobody else wanted it. Grandma Parker was going to keep it for me."

I was full of rage. And her becalmed manner enraged me more. She had done it to spite me, I was sure of it.

"The attic had to be cleaned out." She raised her voice just a bit. "We're moving."

"I know you're moving. To your fancy new house on Main Street. With all the big new rooms and the red damask curtains and the Belgian carpets. It's all you talk about. All you care about."

She turned on me. "Don't you think, Mary Todd, that I deserve a big new house? Don't you ever think how difficult it's been here with all these children in such close quarters? Don't you ever think of anybody but yourself?"

I turned to run and bumped into Pa.

"What's this?" He put his hands on my shoulders to stop me.

"She threw out Ma's clothes. The ones you said I could have. She gave them away!"

"Don't call your stepmother 'she,' Mary. Show some respect."

Respect! I glared up at him. "Don't you care? I wanted to save those clothes. They were all I had left of Ma."

"You have the desk," Betsy put in.

"Yes, and I aim to keep it away from you," I told her.

"Enough, Mary," Pa said.

I ran. As I ran up the stairs to my room I heard Pa asking, "What is wrong with that child?"

"I don't know, Robert, but you'd better rush right out and buy her ten yards of yellow muslin or a new bonnet or some new kid gloves. It's the only way she'll come 'round," Betsy said sarcastically.

THERE IS A HOLE inside me because of the loss of Mama's clothing, a hole I have never been able to fill. I dream, at night, of crossing that attic room and opening the blanket to find nothing. And searching and searching all over the room, with panic inside me, hoping to find it in some deserted corner.

I see her blue taffeta dress, her lace collars, her black shawl, her tea-colored lace blouse. I hold them up in my dreams at night and they disappear in my hands.

THAT SUMMER, as well as the cholera and the confusion of moving, we had the seventeen-year locusts visiting, singing their monotonous song in the background, no matter what was going on.

They were especially loud the day Liz and I brought our things to the new house. It was brick, and Pa had had the whole thing redone so that, except for the large rooms, it no longer resembled Palmentier's Inn.

Those large meeting rooms had been made into parlors. It had six large bedrooms and a two-room nursery and a new piano in one parlor.

All the furniture was new. There was nothing here that had been my mother's, except for the silverware stored in the pantry.

There was a bathtub in the back hall, and in Pa's study at least two hundred books.

I knew, in an instant, that I could not call this place home. I brought my few things upstairs to the room I was sharing with Liz.

"Which bed do you want?" she asked. She was holding Pierre in her arms, deciding where to put him down.

"I don't care. I won't be here that much," I said dismally. "This is your room, not mine. I'm the guest this time."

"You can have the bed near the window," she said generously. "And I wish you were going to be here all the time. I'm going to miss you, Mary."

I nodded and lowered my head. Tears came to my eyes. And then she gave the conversation a new turn.

"Did you know your brother George refuses to come here?"

My head shot up quickly. "What do you mean?"

"He told me so. He said he's not going to leave the old house. He says it's lonely now, and he doesn't want to leave the place where his mother lived."

Oh sweet Lord, I thought. *Now we're going to have trouble.*

AMID ALL THE confusion downstairs, Pa stood, directing the servants where to put things and announcing to all of us that we were having a special supper of turkey and hickory-cured ham and cake from Monsieur Giron's tonight at six, and he wanted us all present to celebrate our first dinner in the new house.

"That includes George," he said. "Mary, go upstairs, find him, and tell him so."

"He's not here," Levi volunteered.

"Where is he?" Pa asked.

"In the old house," Levi said. "He doesn't want to leave."

Pa sighed and looked at me. "Mary, go and talk to him. Tell him what I said."

"Yes, Pa." I walked out the front door slowly.

"Good luck," Levi whispered. And he grinned at me as I went out.

GEORGE WAS SEATED on the stairway when I went in, surrounded by empty space. Why is it that a house looks so sad when it is empty? He looked up at me. "Hey," he said.

"Hey."

Afternoon sun streamed in the windows. Dust motes floated. "You got any food?" George asked.

"For that you have to come to the new house. Pa wants you there. He said we're having a special supper tonight and he wants everyone there. He sent me for you."

In the silence that followed the locusts droned and bounced their sound off the walls. It was eerie.

"You can't stay here, George," I pushed.

"And I'd like to know why not."

"Because Pa will soon sell it, if he hasn't already. New people will move in."

"I can stay until they do."

I sat down next to him. "I know it's hard, leaving. I miss it already, too. This was Ma's house. It remembers her."

He nodded. "That damned Betsy," he said quietly. "If it wasn't for her, Pa would never have moved. Now she wants me in her house, at her table." He shook his head, sighed, and rested his forehead on his drawn-up knees. "Maybe we should run away. Just you and me, Mary. We could join one of those groups of traveling strollers."

It was a tantalizing thought, but I recognized it for the childish dream that it was. So I did not answer him. We sat there like that, together on the stairs, surrounded by empty rooms, for I don't know how long. I calculate it was over an hour. We talked in low tones, about things we'd done in the house. We recalled memories. I was willing to stay like that all night with him if need be.

The light began to change. Still the insects droned. I grew sleepy and hungry and wondered if it was anywhere near six o'clock.

I knew I was in a bind. But I also knew I would never leave George here alone. No matter what happened. I thought to myself, *Pa will come soon. And then we'll leave here. I'm about starved.*

And sure enough, then I heard the crunching of wagon wheels on our front drive. I looked at George. "It's Pa," I said.

I went to the front door and opened it. But it wasn't Pa. It was Grandmother Parker.

SHE STEPPED DOWN from her carriage with a flourish, stood there for a moment looking up at the house as if it were an old friend, then, with the help of her footman, came up the steps and into the foyer.

"What is this?" she asked, holding out her arms. "Are you two camping out here?"

"Grandma, how did you know?" I asked.

She enfolded us in those arms, one at a time. "Because your father sent word to me. And asked me to talk to my two stubborn grandchildren. Mary, you were sent to fetch George, not to encourage him," she scolded gently.

I just sat down again with my brother. "Grandma, he won't leave. And I can't leave him here alone. But I'm beholden to you for coming. I know how hard it is for you to come into this house anymore," I told her.

She nodded and looked around. "This place is haunted," she agreed. "But in a nice way. Yes, it was difficult for me to come here, but I came for you both. I love you and wanted to tell you something."

We both looked at her, expectantly.

"George, your mother is wherever you are, if you want her there. She is always with you. You carry her wherever you go."

George gave her an unwavering stare.

"She's in your eyes," Grandma went on. "You have eyes just like her. Whenever you look at your pa, he sees her. And she's there, in your heart. You couldn't lose her if you tried."

"Is she with me, Grandma?" I asked.

"Yes, child. You have her laugh. Every time I hear you laugh, I hear her. And she is in your mannerisms, even in the way you hold your head."

I had never thought that way before. I got up and hugged her again, burying my face against her dress. "Suppose we didn't have you, Grandma, to tell us these things?"

"Well, you have me. And now I'm asking you to both skedaddle out of here and go to your new home. The time you spend there will be brief enough. Remember, this place could burn down tomorrow and you'd still always have your mother with you. Nobody can take her away from you, no matter how they try."

We skedaddled out of there shortly after that. Grandma got back in her carriage and we headed over to Main Street.

"Imagine her coming to the house to fetch us, George," I said. "Do you know what an event that is on its own?"

"Yes," he said.

"She's stayed away, except for Elizabeth's wedding, ever since Betsy moved in," I reminded him. "It took a lot for her to come for us like that."

"Pa sent her, Mary."

"Nobody sends Grandma anywhere. She wouldn't have come, Pa or no Pa, if she didn't want to. She did it for us."

We continued in silence to the new big house on Main Street. Lights were in all the windows. When we walked in, they were at the table. There were two places empty, one for me and one for George.

George looked at me and I at him. We both saw Pa looking at us from the head of the table. "Come and eat," he said.

Again George looked at me, and I knew what he was thinking. His place was to the right of Pa's and whenever Pa looked at him, he'd see our mother looking back.

We both walked into the dining room and took our places at the table. George never again ate alone in the kitchen.

I KNEW WHAT HAD to be done next before Mammy Sally mentioned it to me. And, as the August light turned mellow at the end of the day, I walked around thinking about it. But I never said anything.

I waited for the right moment to bring the subject up. But Mammy Sally was so busy making the house right after our move that the right time did not present itself.

I was going away to school in little more than a week. The matter not only had to be discussed, it had to be acted upon.

Liz, who knew too much for her own good these days, thought it should be done in the open, with permission from Betsy.

"Just tell her you want to paint some flowers on the fence."

I thought it should be done in secret, that Betsy would never give permission. After all, it was her house now, and she had taken great pains to have the best picket fence installed around the front lawn. She was inordinately proud of it.

"She'll never let me paint flowers on it," I told Liz.

"But you paint so beautifully. I even heard her say so."

I did pride myself on my artwork. At Ward's I had won numerous prizes for it. But my artwork was not the subject here. More was at stake. We'd been in the new house for a week already. What had happened to the runaways that came to our back door on Short Street? How would they know to come to our new house unless given a sign?

Why hadn't Mammy Sally said something to me? Had she given up helping runaways? Had something happened that made her fearful of being caught?

I was determined to ask her that evening. And so, when Frances was at the pianoforte and Pa's new astral lamps were burning in the parlor, I sneaked out into the kitchen where Mammy was kneading dough for tomorrow morning's bread.

"You have nuthin' to do?" She eyed me suspiciously.

"Mammy, I need to talk with you about something."

"Talk away then."

I sat down on the bench next to the table. "Don't you think it's time for me to paint some flowers on the front fence?"

Slap, slap, slap. She patted the dough vigorously, turned it around in her hands, even tossed it into the air, in movements that were at once graceful and mesmerizing.

"Sure is. But jus' 'cause it's time, doan mean it'll be easy. We in her house now," and she gestured with her turbaned head to the parlor where I'd left Betsy at her embroidery.

"I can paint really pretty flowers," I reminded her. "You know how much Pa liked the job I did on the old fence."

"Got nuthin' to do with pretty or not," she said. "What it gots to do with is that she may not want flowers on her white fence. What it gots to do with is, if'n you ask her, she'll say no, jus' 'cause it's you who ask."

"Then I won't ask," I said.

"Oh, what you got planned then? You jus' gonna sneak out there some night and paint? And what you gonna do when she asks who did it? Say it was the debil who painted flowers on the fence with his long green tail?"

"What's happening to the runaways who are coming to our old house," I asked her, "all hungry and tired and lost?"

She lowered her eyes. "I dunno," she admitted sadly. "But it ain't like there's nobody else in town to feed them."

It came to me then. Mammy was afraid. Afraid of being found out, of being sold downriver. It came to me then that it was up to me to paint the flowers on the fence and to take the consequences for my own actions.

"I'll do it," I said bravely. "I'll wait until Wednesday afternoon when she makes her calls. She's gone all Wednesday afternoon. I can do it then."

"You gonna ask your pa first?"

"No. That will only get him involved. He has enough on his mind."

"And when she sees the fence? Then what? You be punished for sure."

I got up from the bench. "I go to school in a week, Mammy. And I come home only weekends. I won't be here anymore." My voice cracked with emotion. "So what can she do to me?"

Was I doing this for the runaway slaves, I wondered, or because I wanted to get back at Betsy for keeping me away from home once school started? And then I had another question. If you were doing a good deed to help someone out, did it matter why you were doing it, just as long as it got done?

But I had no answers for that any more than I had answers for all the other things that plagued me at the moment.

EVERY WEDNESDAY AFTERNOON Nelson brought the carriage, drawn by two of Pa's handsome horses, to the front door where Betsy was waiting for it. Then, all gussied up in his best livery, Nelson would bow in a most formal manner and hand Betsy up into the carriage so he could take her on her afternoon calls.

Sometimes Frances went with her. At such times the silk and satin skirts swished delightfully as they settled themselves in. Then Betsy would give some last-minute order to Mammy, who was still standing on the front steps seeing her off. "We'll have those fresh strawberries for dessert," or "Don't forget, George doesn't leave the house until his sums and penmanship are finished." Then they would be off. And we would have at least three or four hours' time to breathe free.

THERE WAS A HINT of September in the mild August afternoon. Already the sun, though glowing fiercely, did not have the force of summer with it. Stillness sat all up and down our part of Main Street and the leafy green maples and pin oaks kept their watch.

I painted my flowers. Sunflowers this time, with long stalks and faces bursting with mirth. The wooden fence absorbed the paint and it soon dried. I painted a gathering of sunflowers on either side of the pristine white gate. And by the time I could hear the grandfather clock in the center hall ring three, I was finished.

I stepped back and admired my work. It was pretty in and of itself. It needed no other reason for being than its own loveliness. But the reason for its being declared itself. *I'm glad I painted sunflowers,* I told myself as I wiped my hands on my old apron. *Yellow is an easy color to see at night.*

THE AFTERNOON SETTLED into a fearful stillness. I cleaned up my mess and went to the backyard to seek out Nelson for something to take the paint off my hands.

He obliged me without asking any questions. *Slaves know how to survive,* I thought. They know when to speak and when to stay silent. If only I could learn that, I'd stay out of trouble. But we white people never do learn it.

I went up to the room I shared with Liz. She was asleep on her bed, curled up with Pierre next to her. He snored gently. The windows were open and the organdy curtains flapped in a sudden breeze. Outside, on the horizon, dark clouds were gathering. Would there be a storm? I hoped the paint on the fence would dry before there was any rain.

I took my shoes and old apron off and lay down on my bed. Pierre's snores lulled me until I was near asleep.

I lay there, overcome with the enormity of what I'd done.

I'd painted my fool flowers on Betsy's new fence without anybody's permission. It wasn't only that; the flowers had meaning. They were a signal to runaways that this was a safe house.

Should Betsy or Pa find that out, it might result in Mammy Sally being sold downriver. What to do?

There was only one way out. I must behave like one of the servants. I must learn to be quiet. Or when I did speak, I must learn to play the game as they played it. I must outwit them like Brer Rabbit outwitted Brer Fox.

It all came back to me as I lay there. Mammy Sally had taught all of us about Brer Rabbit and Brer Fox.

Brer Rabbit's life was lived in a steady state of war with Brer Fox, who was bigger and stronger, and always out to eat him. I'd grown up on those stories of Mammy's.

"Be polite to Fox as he is to you," Mammy's story went. "Even though you suspect he is plotting to eat you. When he says, 'I'm gonna ketch you,' tempt him with something better. Tell him you know of a man who has a pen full of pretty little pigs, all ready to be eaten. Even though you know that when he goes to that man's house, all he will find is a pen filled with hounds who will chase and kill him."

In other words, she meant, be a trickster. Don't cry and take on. Be smarter than Mr. Fox and you will survive.

I fell asleep, plotting how to be smarter than Betsy. And when I awoke I had the answer.

THANK HEAVENS Pa came home before Betsy. Thank heavens he was there to receive the first of her onslaught when she came into the house.

"Who painted the flowers on my fence?"

She knew, of course, or she would not have been so

irate. She stood there in the front hallway, while people crowded around her. *"Who did this?"*

Frances was with her. So were Ann and Liz.

She called out for Mammy Sally, who came running. She repeated the question, then while not even waiting for an answer, she looked at me.

"Who gave you permission to deface my fence?"

Everyone looked at me. I did not answer at first. Then Pa said, "Mary?"

I stepped forward. "Don't be upset, Ma, please. I did it."

"Why? Who gave you permission?"

Then came my lie, my Brer Rabbit deceit and trickery. "Because I recollected how many compliments you got on the fence in front of our old house. And I know how much you liked the flowers and I thought I'd surprise you and it would make you happy. I only wanted to please you, Ma. That's why I did it."

Silence swirled around in the hallway, thick with possibilities. I looked at Pa. He nodded his head, ever so slightly, in approval.

Betsy was speechless. She did not know what to do. She would receive compliments on the flowers on her fence. She knew that. What could she do?

She handed her silk shawl to Mammy Sally. "I'm exhausted," she said. "I'll have some tea in the front parlor."

THAT VERY NIGHT Aunt Rachel, a runaway, came to our back door.

I heard the rapping and crept downstairs in time to see Mammy Sally lighting the lantern and going outside.

When she saw me, she put her finger to her lips. I nodded yes and sat down at the kitchen table. If anyone caught me, I'd say I couldn't sleep, didn't want to wake Liz, and came down for some warm milk. I got the milk and some sugar cookies and put them in front of me on the table.

In a short while Mammy came back inside. She blew out her lantern and shook her head. "What she wouldda done if I wasn't here this night, I don't know."

She then told me about the woman.

She had no husband. He'd been sold south. Then her children were bought by a planter near Lexington. She was sold to a cotton planter in Mississippi. Wanting to see her children, she escaped and made her way north to Kentucky, surviving on berries and fish she'd caught and eaten raw. She was captured by her master from Mississippi, beaten, and had manacles put around her wrists. Then she and some other slaves were put into a wagon and headed even farther south.

When the wagon stopped she simply got out and disappeared into the woods. She broke open her handcuffs with rocks and somehow found her way north again, aided by slaves on plantations. Now she was here in Kentucky, in our barn.

"She heard that her children were both dead," Mammy told me. "So she has decided to cross the Ohio. If'n we hadn't had those flowers painted on the fence, Lord knows where she would have gone. She's worn down, poor thing. I gave her food and a new shift. Doan worry, Mary. She be gone by mornin'."

Likely, Mammy Sally told me, the woman would be moved to Indiana, once across the Ohio. Then on to Saint Catharines, a settlement in Canada where many slaves fled to.

I went to bed, comforted for the first time in weeks. I was part of something, something more than the petty jealousies and mean-spirited games played in this house.

FRANCES WAS LEAVING. The whole house was in an uproar. She was leaving to live with Elizabeth and Ninian in Springfield, Illinois.

Summer travel was not the best. The roads were dusty or sometimes muddy. But winter travel was impossible, so she was leaving now. Our uncle, Dr. John Todd, who owned a lovely home in Springfield, was escorting her. First they would take the train for Frankfort, then take a stagecoach to Louisville. From there steamboats left twice a week for St. Louis, downstream to the junction of the Ohio and Mississippi at Cairo, then upstream to St. Louis, then to Alton on the Mississippi River.

The last one hundred miles east to Springfield were done by stagecoach, with overnight stops along the way.

If the swarms of gnats didn't get them on the stagecoach trip, then the places where they had to get out and walk through swampy ground would. If the stage wasn't run off the road, if it didn't lose an axle, if rain didn't turn the road to mud, they would get there in two weeks. Often it took three.

Frances was leaving. Into her trunks, which lay open on her bedroom floor now, went all that made up a woman's wardrobe: wrappers, mantles, capes, dresses, skirts, bodices, linings, and undersleeves. Cambric and muslin, satin and velvet, cotton and ribbons, and slippers and boots. Hats and gloves.

Frances was packing up her life, and I didn't know how to say good-bye to her, because we'd had a fight.

Oh, it wasn't over the fact that in two weeks I was leaving the house, too, for school, and nobody even paid mind. It was because of a complete stranger, a sometime friend of hers, the wife of Judge Fielding C. Turner.

As the judge's wife, Caroline Turner was something to be reckoned with as far as society went in Lexington. I know Frances wanted to be like her. But now Caroline had fallen from grace in the eyes of many. Now she was in trouble.

Everybody knew she beat her slaves. But people kept still tongues about it. Some blamed her for the deaths of as many as six of her slaves. But nothing could be proved.

Now, however, everything was out in the open. She had beaten and thrown out of the second-story window her smallest slave, a boy named Jules.

Little Jules was crippled for life.

Her husband had put her in Lexington's lunatic asylum for the last three months, to stave off criminal prosecution. But she insisted on a trial to "clear her name."

Before the trial she was to be examined and questioned

by a panel of six of Lexington's citizens, to determine her state of mind.

Pa was on the panel.

It made for dissension in our house. Frances had already had words with Pa about it. Then with me.

Caroline was from Boston, she reminded Pa. She doesn't know our ways. She was overlenient with her slaves and they became ornery, even threatened to attack her. She was only defending herself. "You know that to be true, don't you, Pa?" she asked.

The only thing he knew to be true, Pa said, was that slavery was tearing his family apart. Why, he knew more than one family in Lexington that had been torn apart by it. "And I don't want it for my own family."

I'd never been close to Frances. She and Ann had always been sisterly, sharing secrets, talking about boys, and doing whatever it was that sisters did. I'd grown up on my own, with only Grandmother Parker and Mammy Sally to confide in.

But now Frances was leaving. I knew, in my heart, as I watched Mammy Sally close the trunks, that Frances would never be back. She was leaving home because of our stepmother. There was no happiness in this home. And she knew it, though she would not admit it.

In Springfield, a raw, unsettled frontier town, she'd find a husband. That was why she was going, wasn't it? When we next met, we'd be grown. She'd be a married woman.

As I watched Nelson pick up the trunks and haul them downstairs where Uncle John was waiting, on the one hand I wanted to throw my arms around Frances. And on the other I hoped it would rain, that the roads would turn to mud, and she'd have to slosh through it. I hoped the gnats would get her.

I stood out front with the others and waved them off. She'll live in the Edwardses' grand house on Second Street, I thought. There will be servants, but there are no slaves in Illinois. No Caroline Turners. And no stepmother. And I envied her, oh how I envied her. For I am left here with all the problems.

So Pa was on the panel, which met every day for two weeks at the courthouse.

We were not to talk about the matter, he said. Not amongst ourselves, not to anyone on the outside, and not to him. It was the same as if he were on a jury, he told us.

Oh, how I longed to speak of the matter to Mammy Sally. As I watched her dark figure move about me, I had to bite the words down on my tongue.

I knew she was weighed down with the matter. All the slaves, in our house and in others, were not only brought low but anxious to know what would happen to Caroline Turner. For, if you could just throw a seven-year-old boy off a second-story balcony and cripple him for life, well then . . .

Well then.

They would not look us in the eyes, any of the negro servants in the house, including Mammy Sally. Lines were drawn. Sides were taken. Silence was the weapon of choice.

As she helped me, in my bedroom, pack my trunk for school, I felt myself teetering on the edge of some precipice. And I knew that if I fell into the blackness, if I left for school without breaking this silence between us, I would lose her forever.

Slavery was tearing us all apart. It was Sunday. Tomorrow I would leave for school. In church this morning our minister reminded everyone how Kentucky's negroes would soon outnumber the whites. And when they did, they would overcome every obstacle, he said. He did not mention Caroline Turner. But he knew that there were at least several members of the panel in the congregation. And he knew there were dozens of negro servants in the gallery, listening. One being Mammy Sally.

Our hands touched now as she folded up one of my skirts and put it into the trunk. For an instant the world stood still. I looked at her.

"Mammy," I said, "don't worry. Pa will find Caroline Turner sane, and then she can face a trial."

"He be not the only one on that panel."

There were tears in her eyes. Tomorrow morning, early, the panel was to meet and come up with its decision.

"Pa will do the right thing," I assured her.

"Don't put it all on your pa. There be a lot of negro unrest. People are scared," she said.

Across the trunk we sought out each other's eyes. She understood! I went around the trunk and ran into her arms.

She enfolded me there and rocked me. "Bad times a-comin', child," she said. "But we always remember our friends."

"I'll be your friend forever, Mammy," I said.

She crooned a song softly, still rocking me. "No matter what, Caroline Turner, she get hers," she said. "God ain't on no panel."

WHEN I LEFT for school the next morning, I left my father's house for good, though I'd be back on the weekends. It was, for me, a final leave-taking. All partings after this would be footnotes in my life. When Nelson lifted my trunks into the carriage, I felt the ropes binding me to home tearing. There was a finality about it that would render any other partings as trivial. These feelings hung heavy on me, and I did not know why.

I think Pa felt it, too. He stood there looking mournful. And well he should. The panel had convened by eight o'clock and was finished at nine, after which Pa came home and told us.

Caroline Turner was free. She was deemed not insane, and somehow she had convinced the rest of the men that she'd been acting in self-defense.

Pa wouldn't discuss the matter. He'd come home, eaten his breakfast, and now he looked as if Brer Fox had him pinned in a briar patch. How much of it was because I was leaving? He was, in a way, losing his third daughter.

The little ones crowded around the carriage and had to be herded out of the way by Betsy and Ann. "Good-bye, Mary, good-bye," they chanted, as if I were off to Springfield, Illinois, and not a mile and a half away.

Liz sat next to me on the seat. Nelson would fetch her home every night. Nobody cared enough to ask me how I would feel, seeing Nelson outside the school every day to fetch Liz, while I stayed inside and didn't go home. Nobody told me how I was supposed to feel. It was all glossed over, as if it made no difference at all.

ROSE HILL WAS the name of the rambling brick structure that housed the school. And it was across the road from Henry Clay's Ashland, which I'd visited a dozen or so times. Why then did I feel, as our carriage pulled up in front, that I'd just finished a two-weeks' journey, that I was hundreds of miles from home?

A whole line of girls waited to meet us, as well as the Mentelles and the servants.

Before I was down from the carriage, Madame Victorie Charlotte LeClere Mentelle came forward, arms open to both of us. "Welcome, welcome. Girls," and she turned to the line of curious onlookers, "this is Mary Todd and her step-cousin Liz Humphreys. Mary is a boarder, Liz a day student. Come now, remember your manners."

I was enveloped in a bevy of chattering, laughing girls. Never mind Liz. I lost her in the shuffle. Never mind my luggage. It would be taken care of by Nelson.

"I'm Mercy Levering," one girl said. She threw an arm around me. "I'm a boarder, too."

"Where are they taking my cousin Liz?"

"Oh, she goes with the day students. You're with us."

"Us?"

I looked at them, at least eight of them, standing around, taking my measure. They were all about my age, all seemed confident and smug, as if they knew some secret I did not know.

"Yes. We're the boarders," Mercy explained. "We all live in that part of the building."

She pointed to a brick wing that jutted out on the left.

"I know where my room is," I said, "I've been here before. I have my mother's ladies' desk here. No one has moved it, have they?"

"It's still safe in the corner where you left it," Mercy assured me. "I made sure no one moved it. I'm rooming with you. Now we just wanted to tell you, that part of the building is for us, the boarders. We live quite a different life than the day students. Don't count on seeing Liz much."

"I've learned," I said tersely, "not to count much on anything."

She met my eyes with her level brown gaze. She seemed to have a mild and thoughtful manner. "You're already one of us," she said. "Come along."

THE HALF DOZEN or so girls who seemed so protective of me were not wearing school uniforms. They each wore their own clothes, dimities, muslins, cotton dresses that most girls our age wore. But it was as if they were all clothed in one color, as if they all were of one species. And now I was one of them.

But what did it mean? What was I?

It was Mercy who told me. She stood in the small room I shared with her and watched as I unpacked my trunk.

"Orphans," she said. "This part of the building is known, here and on the outside, as the house for the orphans."

"Orphans?" I stared at her.

"Yes. None of us has a mother."

I started to speak, then stopped. She was serious. She was grave and dignified and not at all joking. She was dead serious. "I'm not an orphan," I said. I thought of Pa, of my brothers George and Levi, of my sisters Elizabeth and Frances and even Ann. I thought of the little ones I'd left at home.

"I have a family," I told her. "I'm just here because . . ." but my voice gave out.

"Because this is where they put you," she finished. "This is where they put all of us. Because they didn't know what to do with us. So we're here."

She was so accepting about it. But I wasn't. I suddenly lost the urge to unpack. The urge to do anything. Tears were forming in my eyes, I could feel them. *Oh, Pa,* I thought, *no wonder you looked so low this morning. You knew I'd find out about this, didn't you? You really were in a briar patch, weren't you?*

I pushed my trunk aside on the floor and sank down on my bed. Had I been put here because they didn't know what else to do with me? But of course. Elizabeth and Frances and even Ann had their places. Ann knew how to survive around Betsy, something I'd never learned. As for

George and Levi, well, when I left, Levi was asking Pa if he could move to a hotel in town. George still lived in his own world, though he ate at the table with the family. That left just me from Pa's first family.

I lay down on the bed and clutched my stomach as if I were ill.

"Are you all right?" Mercy asked. "Come on, Mary. Somebody had to tell you. It's the same for all of us here."

I turned over, crying. "Leave me be," I said.

SHE LET ME BE and went downstairs. Before she went, Mercy put a coverlet over me. "We're having a special supper to welcome everyone tonight," she said. "It's at six. Rest until then. I'll make your excuses."

It was clouding over outside and fixing to be a real rainy September afternoon. The wind was picking up, forcing leaves from the trees. I dozed.

I was conscious of someone coming into the room and fussing about, but I did not open my eyes. A headache was forming behind them. Lately I'd been getting mind-breaking headaches, and at home Mammy Sally always had some decoction to give me. Here I had nothing. I opened my eyes briefly and saw that someone had placed an astral lamp on my dresser. It gave a pleasant glow to the room.

Just then someone knocked and came in. It was Madame Charlotte.

"Child, what is it? Are you indeed ailing? Or is it homesickness already?"

I sat up. "I have a home," I said to her.

"But of course you do. This is your school."

"Then why am I called an orphan?"

She smiled and sat down next to me on the bed. "Oh, so that's it. We call all the motherless girls orphans. It's how they are known. It's in jest, dear, don't take on so."

"They don't think it's in jest."

She felt my forehead. "You have a slight fever."

I told her about my headaches and she nodded knowingly. "Migraine," she said. "You'll suffer all your life with them if you don't learn to take things more lightly. I can give you some laudanum. Come now, no more crying. We all have a wonderful time here."

"I never have a wonderful time anywhere," I told her. "My life is a disaster."

Her eyes narrowed. "Shall I tell you about my life?"

It was not a question. I was old enough to know when grown-ups asked questions that were not questions. So I nodded my head, yes.

"I WAS THE ONLY child of a wealthy Paris merchant. My father raised me as a boy. My father taught me to ride when I was just a knee baby, and as I grew he made me row, every morning, across the Seine before breakfast.

"I was afraid of death so he locked me in a closet with the corpse of a friend, overnight."

My eyes were wide with wonder. "But you are happy now, aren't you?"

"Yes, child. But my husband and I were forced to flee

across France because revolutionary mobs wanted to burn our children at the stake."

My eyes were drowsy from the laudanum. Was she making up stories as she went along? Just before drifting off to sleep again I heard her say one more thing.

"It isn't what happens to you in life that matters, it's how you take it."

I STAYED FOUR YEARS at Madame Charlotte's. I never went home weekends and every day I could see, from my classroom window, Nelson draw the carriage up front to fetch Liz home from school.

True to Mercy Levering's predictions, I seldom saw Liz in school. She was in a different course of study than I was. I studied French. I read Shakespeare, Sterne, Pope, and Burns. I read and recited poetry.

I always had the lead in our French plays, and when Pa and Betsy and Ann came to see me and pronounced that I was like another person, it was because I was.

I no longer mourned the role assigned to me by Pa, being an orphan. I found pursuits to replace the needs that hole left in my life.

I learned dances, all I would need for my future life, whatever it might be. Evenings Monsieur Mentelle would play his fiddle and his wife would instruct us in cotillions, hornpipes, and all sorts of dances.

The first year I was at the head of my class. Every year following I got the highest marks.

I did talk to Liz during the school year. She told me that Mammy Sally's flowers on the front fence brought a lot of callers.

When I graduated, with the highest honors, Pa gave me money for a whole new wardrobe. And he gave me a trip to Springfield, Illinois, to see my sisters.

EARLY ON A MAY morning I boarded the train for Frankfort, with my cousin John Todd Stuart helping me. He'd come all the way from Springfield to escort me back there. His lawyer business, he said, he'd left in the hands of his new partner, name of Abraham Lincoln.

"Don't expect too much from us," John Todd said to me as the stagecoach approached Springfield. "We're now the state capital, yes, but we're still a frontier village compared to Lexington, Mary. Don't be disappointed."

I was filled with excitement. "Why should I be disappointed?"

"You're such a belle. You're used to concerts and lectures and dances. You're used to shopping in all those beautiful stores you have in Lexington. I'm afraid we have just a handful of dry-goods stores and mail comes only once a week. About eight hundred and fifty people live here. And our streets turn to mud with the first rain."

"Believe me, John, I couldn't be happier than I am right now," I told him.

Then he pointed it out, up ahead on a hill, my sister and brother-in-law's house, a two-story brick affair with a veranda all around it. On the front steps stood my brother-in-law, Ninian Edwards, ready to greet us.

Elizabeth had had a child just one month before. She was still resting. *Well, I can be of help,* I thought, as I climbed down out of the stagecoach. *They won't be sorry they invited me here.*

MY SISTER'S NORTH PARLOR was forty feet long, big enough for all the meetings, teas, and balls they held in it. Since Springfield had become the state capital, it had had an influx of lawyers, and no meeting or gathering took place that didn't happen here. The room was simple yet elegant, with rosewood and mahogany furniture, ornately carved tables, and silver bowls and coffee set inherited from Ninian's father. The Edwardses employed four free negroes at the going wage.

Just as I removed my bonnet and found my way into Elizabeth's arms I noticed, out of the corner of my eye, Ninian lighting a tapered candle in the front window.

No other candles in the room were yet lighted. Ninian smiled at me. "It's a custom we have here, Mary," he said. "We light a candle in the front window to signal the young men of Springfield that there is an eligible young woman at home."

"How many young men?" I asked fearfully.

"Oh, a number of homeless lawyers," my sister Frances said, coming into the room and hugging me. "They've done it to me. Don't worry, Mary. You can abide it. For instance, cousin John's partner, Abraham Lincoln. He calls himself humble Abraham. You'll find him easy to talk to, Mary."

What Happened after Mary Todd Met Abraham Lincoln

MARY TODD met Abraham Lincoln in 1839 in Springfield, Illinois, on her second visit to her sister's. They had a tumultuous courtship with several partings and comings together. Lincoln was shy and awkward, given to moods and depression. But he was a lawyer, a self-educated man who came from pioneer stock and had arrived in Springfield in 1837.

He was completely unschooled in the art of "parlor talk," which included talking to women. Born into a poor farming family, he had only one year of formal schooling. He had worked on a flatboat, as a store clerk, and as a postmaster. He read constantly and could speak fluently by the time he got to Springfield, but he had to borrow money for a suit to attend the legislature.

Yet Mary Todd saw something in this earnest, ambitious, and melancholy man. Of course by the time she met him he had already been elected as town trustee, chosen as a presidential elector at the first state Whig (Republican) convention, and was one of the managers of a cotillion ball at the American House.

After their chaotic courtship, during which Abraham Lincoln almost had a nervous breakdown, they were married in the house of Mary's sister and brother-in-law, the Edwardses.

It was November 1842. Mary wore her sister Elizabeth's white satin wedding dress, which had been Mama's, and a pearl necklace. There were two bridesmaids. An Episcopalian minister married them.

ABRAHAM CALLED HER "Molly" and Mary called him "Mr. Lincoln." They took up residence in the Globe Tavern, a hotel/boardinghouse on Adams Street in Springfield. Room and board cost them $4 a week.

Lincoln was away a lot, riding court circuit (going from county to county to different courts, to try cases). Mary, in time, became pregnant with their first child, who was born on August 1, 1843. They named him Robert Todd after Mary's father.

Her father was so happy that he paid them a visit and gave them $25 in gold and also gave Lincoln a law case that would earn him $50. This money enabled them to start looking for a home.

They found one at Eighth and Jackson streets and settled in. Mary had the help of a black woman named Epsy Smith, who worked for her sister and brother-in-law.

Their second son, Edward, was born in March 1846. In the meantime Mary went on, firmly believing that her husband would surely bring her fame and power.

It was when Lincoln was riding circuit and away from home for weeks at a time that Mary consoled herself with shopping, just as her father used to console her with gifts when things got bad at home.

After working for years for the Whig party, in the fall of 1846 Lincoln was elected to Congress. They moved to Washington, D.C., where they lived in a boardinghouse. But first they paid a visit to Mary's family in Lexington, Kentucky. Here Lincoln saw slavery firsthand, being that Mary's father's house was right up the street from the slave market.

"I bite my lip and keep quiet," he said. He was antislavery.

Lincoln spent two years in Congress. Mary and their two sons returned to Springfield before the two years were up, unable to bear life in a boardinghouse, and Lincoln returned in 1849 when his term was up.

In late July, Mary's father died of cholera; six months later Grandma Parker passed away. In December Eddie fell ill. The Lincolns watched their son suffer with a wracking cough and fevers for nearly two months. Eddie died on February 1, 1850. The Lincolns were devastated. Mary couldn't stop crying, could not eat, and wrote a poem about him that was published in the *Springfield Journal*.

But soon she was expecting another child and this, at least, helped her to stop crying. William (called Willie) was born on December 21, 1850.

Two years later they had Thomas, named after Lincoln's father (called Tad, short for Tadpole).

Lincoln once again was practicing law in Springfield

with the firm of Lincoln and Herndon. Most of his cases were for the railroads, which were advancing and expanding all over the land. Mary spent her time cooking and caring for the children, shopping and sewing and "educating" her husband in such things as wearing a jacket when answering the doorbell and which silverware to use at a dinner party. She kept his spirits buoyed and was a constant supporter in his career, besides being an excellent mother. Both were indulgent parents. Always interested in politics, Mary was soon collaborating with and advising her husband, and there were many people who said Lincoln told them his wife expected him to be president.

Zachary Taylor, a Whig, was in the White House. Lincoln wanted to be rewarded for all the work he'd done for the party. He wanted the post of commissioner of the Land Office. So he went back to Washington to further his cause, and Mary started a letter-writing campaign in his favor to get President Zachary Taylor's attention.

Lincoln didn't get the post but was offered the governorship of Oregon Territory. He declined. They didn't want to live so far away from everything. So for six years his political career came to a standstill. Mary, busy with the children, still continued to bolster his spirits and still spoke of his being president someday.

Lincoln made some speeches (after reading them first to Mary), and in 1858 he entered into a series of debates (seven in seven prairie towns) with Senator Stephen Douglas, Mary's old beau, taking a moderate antislavery position.

Sometimes he spoke as a candidate for the state senate himself, sometimes he spoke for others, but the slavery question was coming to a head and Lincoln knew he had to take a firm position on it. In the late 1850s Lincoln took his stand on slavery, saying in one of his speeches that it was a monstrous injustice.

While still in Springfield, the Lincolns' financial worth escalated. His fame, garnered from his speechmaking, and his influence were expanding. Mary had another floor built onto the house. In the winter of 1857 she threw a party for five hundred people, but only three hundred came because of the bad weather. She was, without knowing it, preparing herself to be First Lady.

But as always, when depressed, she shopped. On one occasion she spent $196.55 for clothing and one of her dresses cost the same as two months' pay for an ordinary Springfield family.

Lincoln continued speechmaking and came to stand for helping the oppressed. He addressed a large audience at New York's Cooper Institute, then traveled to New England where he gave eleven more speeches.

In 1860 he ran for president. War was looming. People predicted terrible results if he won.

In the blink of an eye, when her husband was elected, Mary's life in a fishbowl began. She was finally wife of the president of the United States, something she had wanted since she was a very young girl.

WITH ELEVEN-YEAR-OLD Willie and eight-year-old Tad (Robert had gone off to Harvard), the Lincolns went to Washington. The boys, often called "the Lincoln brats," had the run of the White House.

The Civil War (or War Between the States, as the Southerners called it) broke out in April of 1861. But despite it, Mary continued with her gaiety and parties, which she became known for in the White House. Some of Washington's elite matrons were rude to her—the wife of the pioneer president, the First Lady from the backwoods of Illinois. Others attended her levees (receptions) but talked behind her back.

Those who hated her husband called him "that ape" or "a Black Republican."

As always, when depressed, Mary shopped. She bought a fancy carriage, a 190-piece porcelain dinner set, wallpaper from Paris, silverware, and many other items that overshot the allowance she was permitted to run the White House. To the White House she added furnaces, gaslight, and running water.

She shopped at New York importers, and in Philadelphia. And soon she was criticized for her self-indulgence in Northern newspapers by those who hated her husband.

She interviewed dressmakers to make her lavish gowns. But all those she hired she was displeased with. Fashion was of prime importance to her. On one particular occasion she wanted a "bright rose-colored moiré antique gown," and determined to find just the right dressmaker, she set out to interview three or four more.

Early one morning at the beginning stages of the presidency, a light-skinned black woman walked up to the front entrance of the White House. She wanted the position of dressmaker to the First Lady but didn't think she had a chance of getting it.

Already successful in her trade, and the favorite of Washington's elite, she was a free black woman who had purchased her own freedom.

The interview lasted only a few minutes, and in that time Mary Lincoln hired the free black woman.

Her name was Elizabeth Keckley.

Lizzy

Lizzy—Child of Aggy—Feb. 1818.
Recipe for Muster Day gingerbread. As follows:

AND SO I WAS BORN and my birth registered in the mistress's household diary. I was listed right above the recipe for Muster Day gingerbread. And right below the new shipment of household supplies. "Two bristol boards, a bottle of varnish, a varnish brush, and writing paper."

I was born into the household of Mary and Armistead Burwell of Dinwiddie County, Virginia, on Sappony Creek, south of Petersburg, Virginia's third largest town, where men made money in tobacco factories, mills, and stores.

My birth did not go unnoticed on the large plantation. With every birth of a slave child the master is that much richer. And I suppose that with my mother I would have sold for at least $1,300. Master always said that Aggy, my mother, was worth her salt. It was his favorite expression.

Master was my father, though that was not noted anywhere. For all intents and purposes, my father was a slave from a neighboring plantation, name of George Pleasant Hobbs. I never thought of anyone but Daddy George as my father, though he was allowed to visit us only two times a year, on Easter and on Christmas.

My face is fair and I am light of skin. Somewhere along the years Armistead Burwell got my mama alone, 'bout when his wife was carrying her tenth child, and so I got my fair skin and blue eyes.

Master Burwell inherited Mama and fifteen other slaves when he was only in his teens. She became a nurse for his wife and later their ten children, and so, worked in the big house, and I worked with her.

My mama never spoke to me about how she felt about Master. Or if she had any feelings at all. She did tell me how she grieved because I was a girl. How she regretted not taking the tansy, rue, roots and seed of the cotton plant, the pennyroyal, the cedar berries, and the camphor that could cause an abortion.

She regretted it because a girl child is destined for all sorts of mistreatment at the hands of her master. As it was, any child could be sold away from its mother if they weren't Burwell slaves.

Burwells have never yet sold their slaves off. The slaves on our plantation go back to early colonial days when Master's great-grandfather brought them in tenfold from the docks of New Orleans. Right off the ships from the west coast of Africa, from northern Senegambia. And even the more inland region of the Niger Delta.

Mama says my ancestors were hunters, fishermen, mer-chants, artisans, and farmers. All the slaves on this planta-tion have stories and history to tell.

Mama says that is all fine and dandy. And I should be proud. But I also have to make my own history. Which I have already set out to do.

IF I WERE TO BE SOLD at age four, the price I would
bring, after being weighed on the scale, would be about
$300. A little shady girl like myself isn't worth much. And
then only if I sold along with my mother, whose price
would be about $1,100 because she is such a good nurse
and seamstress.

I already knew that at age four. I heard Massa talk
about it, though I knew he would never sell off me and
Mama. Only planters of no account sell off their own
daughters, although some have been known to do it.

But no matter how much I am worth, here is how I
lived and why.

Me and Mama lived in a cabin in the quarters, where
all the slaves lived on this elegant plantation. We each had
a bed, and the mattress was made of corn shucks, which
was stuffed afresh about once a year. We had a fireplace
with pots hanging in it, ready for cooking, but we never
used it. We always ate in the kitchen of the big house because Mama was nurse to the Burwell children. And there

were ten of them. And she was the one and only seamstress in the whole house.

At four I already knew how to ply a needle. Mama had taught me. I was stitching calico for a patchwork quilt. Mama allowed me to use long straight stitches because they were easier. By the time I was six, I was learning to put together a man's shirt. But I get ahead of myself.

I thought it magic what Mama could do with that needle and wished for the day I would be a seamstress for some grand lady.

But my regular work was not so special. I followed Missus Burwell around. I fetched for her. I stood by her side and fanned away the flies. I did her errands and even went on calls with her, dressed in my finest gingham.

We ate good. We had boiled greens and meat and fish, hoecakes made of cornmeal and cooked on a fire rake. Real butter and molasses. We had pot likker.

The negroes in the quarters got bacon and meal on Saturdays. All week they ate corn and ashcakes, with a little meat on the side. At Christmas they got fruit.

But they were allowed to fish in the creek, something they did at night while fires burned on the edge of the water, in what made the prettiest sight you ever did see. They were allowed to hunt. With dogs, not with guns. When Massa took a fancy to hunt, he would take his two oldest sons with him and some chosen slaves. They went out after possum, coon, and fox. And they took Massa's best hunting dogs to tree the animals.

My grandma was named Sarry. She was Mama's mama and she was the cook, which is part why we got such good victuals in the kitchen. She was also the mistress of the herbs that got given to the slaves when they were sickly. She fed all the little negroes in a trough in the backyard. Nothing fancy, but good rib-sticking food. They ate with oyster shells out of that trough, the oyster shells the only thing that kept them from acting like little piggies.

I ate at the kitchen table with a proper dish and spoon.

The negroes in the quarters get up at four to the blowing of a conch shell by the head overseer, Big Red. They went to the fields when it was still dark and came home after sundown. Or as they say, "From can't see to can't see." Lunch was brought to them in the fields.

We chilluns didn't have many chores, so we hunted for turkey nests and got a tea cake for every one we found. I don't know what those white folk did with those turkey nests. As I got older I pondered it out. They did it to keep us busy or when they wanted us out of their sight.

The slaves all had linsey-woolsey clothing for winter, all spun and made on the plantation's own looms. We house slaves had to make a better appearance so Massa purchased fabric from the Petersburg factory in checks and plaids, and it was soft and pretty to wear.

Sometimes poor white folk from the area would come and stand around the quarters and try to trade with the slaves. They'd trade their calico and snuff for slave food. That's how poor they were. The slaves in the quarters all looked down on them.

I tried not to get sick, 'cause if I did, Grandma Sarry would give me turpentine for a sore throat. As it was, in winter I had to wear a bag of asafetida around my neck to keep away all kinds of ailments. In spring I had to take Jerusalem oak seed in syrup for nine mornings. Grandma Sarry said nine was a magic number and by then I would be rid of the worms.

For headaches she gave me jimsonweed; for warts, nine grains of corn; for measles, corn-shuck tea; for mumps, fresh marrow from the hog jowl. Oh, she knew all the magic one needed to get well. And she was often down to the quarters attending to a sick slave.

I had friends, of course. Jane was one of them. So was Amos. And I can't think of a better way to tell you how things could go bad for us than to tell you their stories.

Oh, yes. We have three drivers on this place. Drivers, or overseers, keep the slaves in line and working. Massa has a rule. The ordinary driver is allowed to give no more than six lashes for an offense. The head driver, twelve, and Big Red, the overseer, twenty-four. Anything can be an offense. And we learn that fast.

I BELIEVE THAT Moses and Solomon in the Bible were negro, that lightning never strikes a sycamore tree because Jesus blessed them, and that springs of water in the ground come from the steps of angels. All these things my mama taught me. And I'll always believe them, because not to believe certain things is to die.

For the first four years of my life I believed in the Burwells. I stopped putting any trust in them after what happened with my friend Jane.

To begin with, it was a bad day on the plantation. When I came to breakfast in the kitchen, Grandma Sarry told me it was a day full of bad omens. "Somethin' about to happen," she said. "You mind yourself today."

I believed her because she was known to sense such things. And sure enough as I sat there at the table eating my hominy and molasses, who came through the door spreading the blue devils but Big Red, the head overseer.

Big Red is so called because of his fiery red hair. And he is over six feet. Mama says she would never want to have to make a shirt for him. He carried his rawhide whip all curled up in his left hand.

I'd never seen Big Red without that whip. I think he must sleep with it.

"It gives him his strength," Mama told me.

At that same time Robert came through the other door, from the corridor connecting the kitchen to the house. At fourteen, Robert was Massa's oldest son.

"Got some coffee, Grandma?" he asked. Everybody on the place called Sarry "Grandma." And she spoiled Robert so. I liked him. He paid special mind to me. Grandma said he spoiled me.

Grandma also said I was never to think of him as a half brother. "Make things more difficult when you both get older," she'd told me.

I'd noticed that Robert paid less and less mind to me of late. Even though he used to favor me when we ran and played in the yard. Robert had taught me to play stickball, checkers, even to know my letters, which I knew better than any white child on the place. He'd sat me on his knee and told me ghost stories.

But now he was fourteen and I was four. And I was a nuisance to him at best, and a trial at worst. He'd become embarrassed if I spoke to him in public, glower at me, and tell me to mind myself and leave him be.

I wasn't wanting to be a trial to any of the white folk. I'd leave him be if that was what he wanted. But I still looked up to him and worshipped him.

He and Big Red exchanged greetings as if Grandma and I did not exist.

"Mornin', Big Red," Robert said.

"Mornin', Master Robert."

So now. Something else had changed. Big Red, who answered only to Massa, had taken to calling Robert "Master." Well then.

"I got some bad news," Big Red said.

Robert nodded, as if bad news was to be expected and he could abide it without a wink.

"Sit down," Grandma Sarry told Big Red. "Have some coffee and put down that whip."

Big Red sat. He put down his whip. Grandma was the only negro on the place who could order him about, or order anyone about, for that matter.

Grandma put a dish of hoecakes in front of him. And some coffee.

"You found Basil," Grandma said.

Big Red nodded. Basil, an important negro on the place because he could do so many things, had gone missing last night. There had been a terrible rain during the night, the Devil's own, Grandma called it, cold and slashing and unforgiving.

"He daid?" Grandma asked. She was not afraid to steer things along, even in front of Robert. She'd boxed his ears many a time and he was still afraid of her.

"Yeah," Big Red answered. "I found him in the creek this mornin' floating facedown."

"Anybody tell Hannah?" Hannah was his mother.

"No. I was hopin' you would," Big Red answered.

Grandma just nodded and sighed, pushed me, and told me to stop staring. I went back to my hominy and molasses.

If I was good, Grandma would give me a little coffee later, very little with lots of milk and sugar. I loved her coffee.

"What was he doin' near that creek in this weather?" Grandma said.

"Ran off," Robert put in. "To Bartlett's likely, to see his wife, Lily."

Lily worked for the Bartletts, two miles down the road. Basil was allowed to visit her only once every few months, but he ran off regular-like to his wife.

"And last night he had to cross the creek to get home," Big Red put in. "He couldn't swim."

"What did you do with the body?" Robert asked.

"Outside, in the wagon," from Big Red.

There was silence for a moment while Grandma attended to the pots hanging in the fireplace and Robert and Big Red talked small talk about the funeral, which was to be tonight.

Then, of a sudden, Big Red looked at me. "How old is she?" he asked Grandma.

"All of four," Grandma answered.

"Old enough to pick worms off tobacco leaves." He stated it flatly. Then said to me, "You sickly, girl?"

"Her name is Lizzy," Grandma said.

"What you good for, Lizzy? Just settin' around and eatin' all day? Or do you work?"

"She's my mother's girl," Robert put in.

"Can't she talk for herself? She dumb or something?" he pushed.

"Talk, Lizzy," Robert ordered.

"I fetch for Mistress," I said. "I serve her. I'm four."

"She isn't ever going to work in the fields," Robert told him flatly. "She's special."

"What makes her special?" Big Red asked.

Nobody said anything. But the silence was so full you could feel it. And then Big Red said, "Oh, oh I see, another one of the master's special ones." Then he got up and walked to the door that led into the corridor to the house. "Too many special people around here if you ask me."

"Nobody's askin'," Grandma said. "Why don't you go into the dining room and tell Massa 'bout Basil. He'll want to know."

Big Red harrumphed and left.

"You'd best go to breakfast with your family, Robert," Grandma told him. "Or I'll hear it again 'bout your hanging around the kitchen and eating."

He got up. He did not look at me. But he said something. "Long as I'm around, you won't be picking worms off tobacco," he said. And then he went into the house.

We went to Basil's funeral that night, but before the funeral, before night fell, something else happened on that blue-devil day. And it concerns my friend Jane.

LATER ON THAT DAY word went around the place, the way it goes through the quarters like a dry hot wind, that Massa had given Big Red what for because of the loss of Basil. It was Big Red's fault that Basil had run off again, Massa said. Never mind why or how. It just was. Most everybody on the place knew to stay clear of Big Red and his curled-up whip that day. But my friend Jane couldn't help it. She was right there, in front of his face in the fields.

JANE WAS JUST ten years old and the kind of friend you could tell anything to. She was more like a sister, but though I had half sisters aplenty in Massa's house, I'd die before I'd tell them anything, much less talk to them. All of Robert's sisters were prissy-boots and like a gaggle of giggling geese.

When we played around the quarters with the other slave chilluns and Massa's white chilluns (yes, they played with us, too), Jane always looked after me, especially in those days when Robert didn't come to play anymore. She had to look after me. Too many times Mikey, Big Red's little boy, hit me with a stick or shoved my face in the dirt. I dared not do likewise to him, just because he was Big Red's boy, but that was no account to Jane. She roughed him up a couple of times, so he left us crying. Nothing was ever said or done, until that day.

I didn't know of it until after sundown when I went to the quarters to see who was about to play with. The chilluns were playing all right, but Jane wasn't there. I asked around and Mikey spoke up. "She's a sissy-boots, always cryin'," he said.

The other chilluns told me where to look, and so I went to find her. Sure enough, there she was behind the washhouse, bawling like a stuck pig and throwing up.

"Jane, are you ailing?"

She waved me off, but I stayed.

"Should I get Grandma Sarry?"

She gulped back her tears and wiped her eyes with the corner of her apron. "Yes, no, I dunno. Ain't nothin' she can do for me."

Then she told me what happened. "He made me bite the heads off all of the worms."

"Who? What worms?"

"Big Red. This afternoon. I was workin' in the tobacco fields. He said I left some worms on the leaves and he called me over and made me pick them off and bite their heads off and swallow them."

My world whirled around. I felt sickly myself then. I could think of nothing to say so I went to her and hugged her. "Come on with me in the house. Grandma Sarry will fix you up."

"I don't want to swallow turpentine."

"No. I'll ask her to give you candy," I said with all my four-year-old reasoning.

Jane was never the same after that. No more did she protect me against Mikey. And there was nothing either of us could do.

Grandma Sarry did give us both candy that night. Fresh-rolled taffy. And then we had to go to Basil's funeral so she gave us both lightwood torches.

Slaves are always buried at night. It's the only time we have to mourn proper-like. All Massa's negroes are buried in a beautiful grove full of evergreens. We sang our sad and broken songs. Basil's wife did not come to the funeral. I do not know if, at that time, she even knew he was dead.

ALL THE TIME, even on the best of days, even when the slaves sang in the fields and had corn shuckings and weddings, we were threatened with the specter of the negro buyers. They came from Petersburg. And once in the hands of the negro buyers, we would be taken and sold South, where we would never again have our hominy and molasses. Where we would have to eat cottonseed to survive.

If I was sold down South, I would, as soon as I was old enough, be in the fields from before sunup till after sundown. Maybe picking worms off cotton or tobacco and being made to bite off the heads of the ones I missed and eat them, by a driver ten times worse than Big Red.

I HAVEN'T TOLD YET about others on our plantation. Oh, there were dozens of slaves, so I can't name them all. But the ones that were important to me are as follows:

There was Uncle Isom who was old but still worked. He made the shoes for everybody on the place and told stories to us little ones when we visited his shed.

There was Aunt Charlotte, who was really my aunt because she was my mother's sister. She was personal maid to Mistress, and she had three daughters, Amy, Hanna, and Lucy, who all did housework and waited on the table. Even though it was the unwritten rule on plantations that house servants be mulatto, Aunt Charlotte had somehow convinced Mistress that Amy, Hanna, and Lucy were handsome enough to work in the house. So they slipped into their jobs by the skin of their teeth, and they seemed to know it. Seemed to know that with one offense they'd be out in the hot fields all day, hoeing and digging and picking. And they just out and out hated me because I was so light skinned. And never missed a chance to let me know it.

Of course, there was another rule. That house servants never fight. And this they knew, too. I could tease them all I wanted when they were mean to me. And they couldn't do a thing about it. Because if they hurt me in any way, they'd find themselves in the fields.

"Massa's little darling," they called me. Though I couldn't see that I was favored.

Then we had Minna's Ralph. Minna worked in the fields and her thirty-year-old son Ralph was what the slave traders would call a "prime nigra." He was strong and a good worker. His back had never been touched by a whip. He bore no scars like so many of the other men did. At the slave sales in the old market in Petersburg they'd put him up on the block and bid him off just like they'd do with the best racehorses, and Ralph knew it.

Ralph knew that he'd bring $1,500 for Massa. If Massa ever needed $1,500, he'd be the first to go.

So Ralph wanted to run. But he needed money. And he found it in the pocket of Massa's jacket when Massa took it off one day in the barn.

Massa was wild with anger. But I think he was more scared. It's one thing to have lazy nigras, it's another to have nigras who steal.

So here is what he did. He gathered us all together in the quarters. I saw Minna's Ralph. He was on the edge of the crowd when Massa had one of the nigras bring out a small coop. In it was his best rooster, who was as mean and wily as old Brer Fox.

That old rooster's name was Belshazzar, like the last king of Babylon that Grandma Sarry told us about. Then Massa had us all line up and file past Belshazzar's cage and stick a finger out at him.

The one Belshazzar bit would be the one who stole the money, Massa said.

And that person would be whipped.

I remember standing in front of Mama and feeling her

hands on my shoulders and hearing her whisper in my ear not to worry. "Nobody gonna hurt you while I'm around."

Well, I knew that wasn't true. I knew if Mistress took it in her head to whip me, nobody could stop her. Not my mama, or even Daddy George if he was around. And it made me mad that Mama would even say such.

Then, before we even got near Belshazzar, Big Red, who was pacing up and down with his whip, noticed that Minna's Ralph was missing. He wasn't in that line, or anywhere near it. So they knew that Minna's Ralph was the one. Else he wouldn't have gone missing.

We don't get near the papers. They don't come to the quarters. But they come into the house. And Mama read it to us. An ad in the *Petersburg Intelligencer* advertising a reward for the return of Minna's Ralph, a thirty-year-old buck from Sappony Creek way, who'd run off on his master.

We who knew of the ad told others. And everyone waited. First days, then weeks for the return of Minna's Ralph. But he never came back. Somehow that money must have gotten him into the Underground Railroad. And by a month later he was likely up North.

And I didn't tell you about the most important one of us yet. So I will now.

Amos was just three, and the darlingest baby on the place. He ran around free, playing in and out of the house, the quarters, anywhere he wanted to go. He was in that part of his life where he didn't know he was a slave yet. Where he thought the whole world was his.

Lots of times I played with him. I was teaching him his letters when the bad thing happened to Amos.

Master was short of money. Word went around in whispers from slave mouth to slave ears. It was September and Massa had just purchased his hogs for the winter and he didn't have the money to pay for them.

He owed $400. A lot of money. Four hundred dollars was the going price now for a healthy young slave child. Everybody on the place knew it. And so Jane and I were told to walk quietly, with downcast eyes. To be near as we could to invisible. You don't have to teach a slave child how to do that. We're born knowing how to make ourselves invisible.

Except Amos. He wasn't about to walk. He had places to go so he ran. He could never keep those bright brown eyes of his downcast. They were looking straight out at the world, daring anyone to stop him.

He called me "Wizzy" because he couldn't say the letter *L*. He was the fifth of his mother Lana's six children. One baby came after him. Lana was the laundress.

So there is Amos, running around to beat all Satan's underlings, and there is Massa looking around and wondering where he's gonna get $400. And his eyes light on Lana and he figures, "She's got six of 'em. She won't miss one."

So he sends word down to the quarters that Lana is to clean and dress Amos and send him to the big house. I greeted him when he climbed the front steps, all spiffed up and smiling. I took his hand and led him into the parlor like I was told to do. I sat him down and kept him quiet. We practiced our *ABC*s.

Massa was in his study, offering some whiskey to the man who'd come half an hour earlier. I knew who the man was. The slave trader from Petersburg.

I don't know what I expected. That he'd be wearing horns and carrying a pitchfork, I suppose. I was surprised to see a well-dressed man in broadcloth, neat and polite and kind, when he walked through the door.

"Wizzie?" Little Amos looked at me wide-eyed. He knew something was wrong.

He put his little hand in mine and I held it. And we sat in silence until the door of Massa's study came open and the two men appeared.

The slave trader walked over to us. "Which one?" he asked Massa.

"The boy," came the reply.

"That's a likely girl you've got there. Good-looking. You wanna throw her in the deal and make another $400?"

I held my breath. Did Massa hesitate just a heartbeat? He did. And then he smiled and said no. "Can't. Not her. She's special."

Amos still clung to my hand as we followed Massa and the slave trader outside. "Just for the fun of it, let's see what he weighs," the slave trader said when he sighted the scale by the smokehouse. "See how much you're getting a pound."

And he lifted Amos and set him on the scale and weighed him, like you would a pig or a side of bacon.

All around us slaves had gathered, in quiet agony, arms folded across their chests. I heard a wail, and without turning knew it was Amos's mother, and that she was being held back by other women as the slave trader carried Amos over to his waiting wagon and put him in.

Quickly his carriage went down the road. And Amos sat in it, in his best clothes, not even knowing what was going on.

Massa turned away from the long hard looks of his slaves and went into the house. Now he had his $400. Now he could pay for his hogs.

After Amos was sold off, the rest of us chilluns knew we'd never be safe again.

I started to have fears in the middle of the night. I'd hear a *tap-tap-tap*ping on the window and jump up out of bed and look for Amos.

When Mama came to get me I'd say, "He's come back. Let him in. He can't stay out there."

Needless to say I started looking sickly. Grandma Sarry saw that my face was swollen and said I had a case of the mumps. She was all ready to give me marrow from the fresh jowl of a hog when Mama stopped her. Couldn't she see my face was swollen from crying?

Aunt Charlotte's Amy, who was sick to the teeth of dusting, said I needed some chores to do in the house to take my mind off things. Her sisters agreed.

Massa, who couldn't abide one of his slaves being sick, said he had the cure.

"What be that?" Mama asked him.

"She needs to see her daddy," he said.

Now that may sound a bit peculiar because anybody who had the brains God gave a hooty owl knew that Massa was my daddy. Though he never admitted it and it was not spoken of. We all knew he was speaking of Daddy George.

I loved Daddy George, who knew how to be a daddy better than anybody. He was better even than the marrow of a hog's jowl for what ailed you.

And so it was that Massa Armistead Burwell got on his horse and rode the two miles to see Mr. John Sampson, who owned Daddy George. And convinced him to let Daddy George come and visit us.

"My little Lizzy."

Daddy George held me on his knee. "You know, I can't decide who I love better, my daughter or my wife."

I knew he wanted to talk to me about Amos being sold away. But I also knew he couldn't.

He couldn't because he couldn't promise "it'll never happen again." Or, "If I was here, I wouldn't have allowed it."

And I, for all of my five years, knew this. Knew there was nothing he could say that would make amends.

Instead he smiled at me, showing even, white teeth, and said, "I'm here for a whole two days. We'll go fishin' together."

And so we did. And when he left, he made no promises. He just told me, "Learn your stitchin', Lizzy. Learn your book."

It was all he had to give me, and all I really needed as it turned out in the end.

GRANDMA SARRY TOLD me once that she thought our massa had abolitionist leanings. Then she had to explain to me what an abolitionist was. When I heard, I nearly went daft.

A fine Southern gentleman like Massa wanting to free his slaves? People did that? Who would serve Massa's morning coffee? Who would shave him? Who would iron his white ruffled shirts? Did they have people to do such things for you up North?

I don't know how much I understood about the whole thing. But I can say that the next time I laid eyes on Massa I looked real close like to see if he leaned in a special way.

Yes, he did. It seemed his head leaned a little to the right when he sat down. So he did have leanings after all.

THE SOIL ON Massa's plantation was getting tired, Robert told us. He told us about the yellow sandy fields as if they were old friends who were too worn down to work. "So we can't plant any more tobacco on them," he explained.

"So we'll have to move."

There were times when Massa sent Robert, his eldest son, to break bad tidings to us. Because he didn't know how.

Robert always did a good job of it. He'd stand there tall and manly in front of us and look us right in the eyes and deliver his message. Robert was growing up fast. He looked every inch the young master of the place. He could even make Grandma Sarry mind, and she'd all but brought him up.

But Robert was going away in the fall to Hampden-Sydney College in Prince Edward County. It was seventy miles southwest of Richmond, he told us.

My mama, who was as expert at tailoring as she was at dressmaking, had sewn him a fine new set of britches and coat, and many white ruffled shirts for him to wear.

"Move where?" Mama asked him now.

"To Hampden-Sydney, where I'm going to school. My father will tell you all about it."

"When do we go?" I asked.

Robert smiled at me and patted my head. "I go in a week. You all will follow directly. Don't worry. It will be good for everybody."

"Is Massa gonna take us all?" Grandma Sarry asked.

Robert hesitated. "No," he said.

"Is he gonna start sellin' his people off then?" Grandma pushed.

"You-all have nothing to worry about," Robert said again. Then he turned and left the kitchen.

———

MASSA SOLD OFF all of his livestock and most of his slaves. In the next week the plantation was crawling with people poking their noses into every nook and cranny and arguing loudly about the worth of things and the best way to manage nigras.

"I'll tell you what," I heard one beefy-looking man who must have been a driver say, "you can manage your ordinary nigra by lickin' 'em and givin' 'em a taste of the hot iron once in a while, but if a nigra sets himself up against me I got no patience with him. I just draw my pistol and shoot him dead and that's the best way."

I stayed out of the way, but I did get to see the slave sale. Never in all my born days did I ever see the likes of such. I stood wide-eyed while person after person that I knew was brought up to stand on the wooden platform in the yard.

The buyers crowded around the stand and the slave trader, Mr. Pfeiffer from Petersburg, started speechifying.

"These are the terms of the sale. One-third cash, the rest to be paid in two equal installments bearing interest from the day of the sale."

The buyers numbered about fifty. Men of every cast from young fancy-pants gentlemen in high-polished boots and perfect cravats to crude-looking drivers like Big Red and elderly refined gentlemen like Massa.

I heard the words "prime" and "strong" and "faithful" a lot about the men. And "sleek" and "good breeder" and "likely little piece" about the women.

Tears came to my eyes as Big Red led Lana to the platform with her remaining five children.

"What do I hear for chattel number forty-four? A healthy, hardworking washwoman with or without the little ones? It's up to you, folks."

The "little ones" clung to Lana's skirt. The baby clung to her neck. And she stared straight ahead, looking at no one, her eyes filled with tears.

"Do we start the bidding for the whole lot?" Mr. Pfeiffer was asking. "What do I hear for the whole lot?"

Someone in the crowd offered $300 and Mr. Pfeiffer laughed. "Come on, folks, this could be the buy of the day, but let's show a little consideration here. The woman here is a fine article without blemish, not to mention how she'll wash your shirts." And he gave a low laugh. "The little nigras will soon be old enough to pick the cotton in your fields."

The bidding got serious and went on and up. And I felt myself entering into the spirit of it if only to see Lana go with her children.

In the end the children went for $400 each. Lana went for $1,500. So in all Massa made $3,500 on Lana and her family.

I turned my back as Lana's new owner, a gentleman in a white neck cloth and gold-rimmed spectacles, led her away. He looked kind. And she'd sold with her whole family. That was more than we could hope for.

"Come on," Grandma Sarry said. "I have some nice milk and cookies. This is no place for a sweet little girl like you."

Here are the names of Massa's other children, who are my half brothers and half sisters.

The boys are Robert, John, Armistead, Benjamin, Charles, and William. The girls are Anne, Mary, and Fanny.

The boys all treated me like a sister. I played with them in the yard and in the house. I sat and learned with them when their tutor came. I was the only "shady" child on the place to be taught to read and write. Because my father was Massa, I had privileges.

On the other hand, the girls were quicker and mean. They knew what my position was and never missed a chance to order me around. And I had to obey them.

They saw things straight and smart. Like the time we were sitting around in the parlor, just talking. The girls were supposed to be doing their embroidery. I was supposed to be stitching a piece of calico for a quilt.

"You can't stitch very well, and your own mama a seamstress," said Mary.

"Her own mama is more than that," Fanny put in.

"What does that mean?" Mary asked innocently.

Fanny giggled. "Well, just think of it this way. Our papa is her father but not her daddy. I don't know how else to put it."

"Then don't put it any way," said Anne, the oldest. "It's something we're not supposed to talk about. Mama doesn't even say such words."

"You know what I heard Sally Olsen from over the creek say?" Mary pushed.

"What?" they asked.

"Every plantation has their own share of shady babies on the place. The mistress never acknowledges it, but she talks aplenty about the shady babies on the plantation down the road."

"Get back to your embroidery," Anne ordered.

But Mary insisted. "Just because you're special around here doesn't mean our daddy is yours," she told me. "So don't think you're so important."

"I don't think I'm important," I said.

"Good. 'Cause all shady babies take their mother's condition, and that's slavery. So you can wear all the calico dresses you want, and eat the same food as we all do, and read and write your eyes out, but you'll never be like us."

I don't know what all would have happened if Mistress hadn't walked into the room then. But she did and the conversation was interrupted. But not finished. I didn't think for one minute that it was finished. And I worried about the day it would be taken up again.

They knew my mama's place in the scheme of things, too; knew Massa attached importance to her words, listened to her, and had many conversations with her. And they went to her instead of their own mama for many things. This made Mistress angry, of course, and so we were all caught up in the swirl of things that were not of our own making.

Sometimes, in the mix-up of people in the house and the closeness of us all, Mistress got confused. Like the time she gave Aunt Charlotte, her personal maid, her best silk dress to wear. Because they were so close, mistress and maid, did Mistress think she was one of her own?

Nobody knows, but it caused a set-to, one of the last before we left the plantation.

That first Sunday in September, it was, now that I recollect correctly. Time came to go to church. We nigra household servants were allowed to accompany the family because the pastor always told the nigras in the balcony to "be good and obey your masters."

We were all ready, waiting in the parlor, when Mistress came down in her robe. "I can't find my good silk," she told us. "Where is my maid? Where is Charlotte?"

"You gave the silk to Charlotte, Mama," said Anne, the oldest. "I saw her all dressed up in it, ready for church."

"I let her try it on," Mistress said. "I never gave it to her."

"Yes you did, Mistress." Aunt Charlotte came into the room then, looking like a blue jay in the blue silk dress.

"Well, don't you look fine in that dress, Charlotte," Massa said in that low refined voice of his that bespoke quality.

"Better than I do?" Mistress asked.

Everyone was silent until Massa said, "Why no, dear, of course not."

As it turned out, though, Aunt Charlotte did look better. She just plain and simple filled out that dress better. Mistress was skinny. And the color looked beautiful against Aunt Charlotte's burnished skin. She looked like a flower just bloomed.

"Give the dress back, Charlotte," Massa ordered.

They went upstairs, and when Aunt Charlotte came down, she was wearing her old plaid linsey-woolsey. And in church I saw Mistress crying.

I tell this to show how close we house nigras were to Massa and Mistress. We entwined with each other, like ivy on a trellis, each strand reaching for the same sky, sometimes comforting and doing for each other and other times bickering and fighting. Like a real family.

Mayhap my elders had pondered it out, but I didn't. There were times when I felt like family, and all I would have needed was Daddy George to make things complete.

I know for a fact that Massa tried to buy Daddy George from his master before we left. He wanted to bring Daddy George with us. So he must have felt the same way. But Daddy George's master wouldn't sell him.

MASSA WAS GOING to be something important at Hampden-Sydney. They called him a steward. The people who ran the place wanted him because he was "moral, kind, and affectionate," they said.

Massa's job was going to be to feed the hungry students. Grandma Sarry was going to cook along with Aunt

Charlotte's three girls, and Massa was bringing along other women slaves he could afford to keep, to serve. The men he kept were few, but they would cut the wood for the fires in the kitchen and the boys' rooms, care for the carriage and horses and cows and dogs and chickens that would be ours, and keep the garden.

There were 140 students. Massa would be busy.

"Some of the students bring their own nigras from home," Massa told us, "and they'll have to be fed, too."

My duties were to be the same as before. Follow Mistress around and carry and tote and fetch for her. Then, the day before we left, she called me to her.

"How would you like to be personal nurse to a new baby?" she asked.

"Yes, ma'am." Whose baby? I did not ask. I knew enough to keep a still tongue in my head.

"Massa and I are expecting another little one," she said. "And when she comes you can be her personal girl. You can belong to her. Wouldn't you like that?"

Like I said, I know when to keep a still tongue in my head. So I said yes, I would like it very much.

THE BURWELLS WERE to live in a two-story brick house right next to the Common Hall. Behind the house were the quarters, where we nigra servants lived, just like back home only smaller. Mama and I again shared one log cabin.

It had red mud in the cracks between the logs. The roof was made out of regular boards that had so much space between them that when it rained we had to move our bed. And at night I could look up and see the stars through those boards.

Our bed ticks, or mattresses, were stuffed with wheat straw. Some of our people slept on rye or oat straw. The fireplace was a good size and even though we ate at the big house, Mama always kept a fire going with 'taters and corn pone roasting in the ashes for anybody who might want to stop by.

We didn't see much of Robert since he went to the Theological Seminary part of the college. Robert wanted to be a minister. But shortly after we arrived it was his birthday so Grandma Sarry made him a special cake. Aunt Charlotte's daughters Amy, Hanna, and Lucy brought it into the dining room with me in tow. We brought it right to his table. And that sweet-talking Robert didn't have a thing to say, he was so surprised.

"Are these your slaves, Robert?" one of his friends asked.

"In so many ways they are like family," Robert said.

The other boys at the table hooted at that. "Well said, old man. I couldn't have put it better myself," one called Josh said.

They called Robert "Old Man," because he was so serious.

THE COLLEGE CHURCH had a new pastor by the name of Reverend J. D. Paxton.

We all went to his Presbyterian church of a Sunday, where he reminded us slaves of the importance of our faith. He talked right at us, telling us to be patient and obedient. He was a kindly man who had a dozen slaves of his own.

It didn't take us servants in Massa's house long to see that Paxton's slaves were better clothed than we were. Even his older boys, who measured out and fixed the stock feed and fetched in wood and water, had good sturdy trousers to keep them warm and not just long linsey-woolsey shirts and ragged pants. The women and girls wore fringed shawls to church and had poke bonnets with ruffles around them. Their dresses looked store-bought while ours, also store-bought, looked shabby in comparison.

Their chillun slaves were all the time sucking peppermint candy, and they told us about Raw Head and Bloody Bones who lived in the woods and waited to eat up little chilluns.

One day, after we had been there about six months, the Reverend's chillun slaves told us that they would soon be free, that they were going to a place called Liberia in Africa.

Their names were Alma, Francine, Allie, and Joan. The boys were Hal and Jupiter.

"Free, free, free," they chanted in front of me and Jane and Aunt Charlotte's girls. "We're goin' home."

"You got no home there," Jane told them. "You never lived in Liberia."

"We all do," said Joan, the oldest. "Reverend says he sees the error of his ways. He says he is having a crisis of conscience. Whatever that is. And he can't make it right in his heart to keep us anymore."

The rest of us did not know what a crisis of conscience was, either. But we understood the all of it, all right. Reverend Paxton and his wife had joined something called the American Colonization Society. These people freed their slaves and had set up a colony in Liberia for them to go to.

For a while everything went along the same. Winter came and went and then one day when I was helping Grandma Sarry in the kitchen garden, Allie, Francine, Alma, and Joan came through the gate.

They were all gussied up in their store-bought dresses and ruffled bonnets.

"We came to say good-bye," Joan told us. "We're leaving."

I noticed, beyond the fence and in the road, the Reverend's carriage. And there he stood waiting with his wife and Hal and Jupiter.

"You're leaving?" I couldn't believe it. "Just like that?"

"Master freed us," said Joan. "We're going with him and Mistress to meet the people who will take us to Liberia."

"We're going on a boat!" Alma's eyes were shining.

Free? The word went into my mind and whirled round and round, but found no place to rest. It was not understood, not welcomed. *How do you get free?* I wondered. "Can you be a slave one minute and free the next?" I asked.

"Master has to free you," Joan said. "He has the important mens make out papers. Only our master can do it because he's a reverend."

I must have looked like my spirit was on the ground because Grandma Sarry put a comforting arm around my shoulder. The girls left. I stood watching at the gate until the carriage was out of sight.

"It's not that your massa has to be a reverend to free you," Grandma said.

I looked up at her.

"Any massa can do it if he takes it in his mind to," she explained.

"Will our massa ever send us back to Africa, Grandma?"

"Don't count on it, child. There's only one way to get free if you want it bad enough."

"Run?"

"That, too. Only there's too many dangers in that. A better way is to be patient, like the reverend says. Learn your sewing. Learn your book. And grow up being extra special at something. Then have Massa hire you out and get paid for your services and save some money so you can buy your own freedom."

"Buy my own freedom?" Never had I heard such a thing.

"Buy yourself," she said. "Your daddy is trying to do just that right now, don't think he isn't. He's got his master to agree to hire him out so he can make the hundred and twenty dollars a year he needs to buy his own freedom and come to us."

"Oh, Grandma!" I hid my face in her skirt. "How can I do it?"

"First you grow up," she said. "And then if'n you still want it bad enough, you'll find a way to do it." And with that she turned and went back to the garden.

I forgot to tell how, when we left the plantation, Massa did two things that turned out bad for us.

He brought along Big Red to oversee his slaves and he purchased Uncle Raymond, Mama's brother, who was at the same plantation where my daddy lived. I like to think he purchased Uncle Raymond for Mama's sake, because he couldn't purchase my daddy.

Uncle Raymond was a man of good parts. He was gentle and he laughed a lot, and once at Hampden-Sydney he taught us chilluns to dance. He played the banjo and taught us the turkey trot and the buzzard lope and the Mary Jane.

He taught us to hold hands and dance in a ring, to sing, *"You steal my true love and I steal your'en."*

The men and women usually joined in, carrying big, fat lighted torches of kindling wood while they danced.

In no time at all Uncle Raymond became uncle to every child on the place, nigra and white. That is, when he wasn't doing his job of making bricks.

There was building going on at the college, and when

Massa brought along Uncle Raymond he right off hired him out to the college to make bricks out of the red clay that was all around.

He had to keep all the farm tools in order, too. Part of those tools were harnesses and plow lines.

In spring, around about April, Uncle Raymond lost a set of harnesses. Massa gave him a new set and told him that if he lost those he would be punished real bad-like.

All I can say is that Uncle Raymond must have known a side of Massa that the rest of us never knew about. Because of how it turned out in the end.

EVERY MORNING WHEN Mama got up, she took a bucket and walked down to Dry Fork Creek to get some water to wash herself with.

One morning we heard her outside, screaming. I was in the kitchen with Grandma Sarry, having breakfast.

"That's your mama," Grandma said, and she ran out the kitchen door.

I ran out after her. And sure enough, there was Mama running up the hill from the creek, her skirts all flapping and her hair all askew. You'd think Raw Head and Bloody Bones were chasing her.

"Child, what is it, child?" Grandma yelled.

"Raymond," Mama sobbed. "Oh, Mama, he's dead."

"Dead? How? Why?"

"What happened, Aggy?" A door slammed and Massa came out of the residence.

"Raymond. Oh, Massa, he done kilt himself. He done hang himself on the tree down by the creek."

UNCLE RAYMOND HAD lost the second set of harnesses. "He hanged himself rather than be punished the way Massa punishes his servants," Grandma said.

As it turned out in the end, we found that the harness had been stolen. Big Red found the man who stole it, a nigra who was not punished for it because everybody was in an uproar over Uncle Raymond.

Mama never again took up her bucket in the morning and went down to Dry Fork Creek to get her water. I had to do it for her. But after that I learned that there were better fears to have than Raw Head and Bloody Bones. And they were the people all around us all the time.

THEY CUT Uncle Raymond down and washed him good and wrapped him in a winding-sheet, then laid him on a cooling board where he would stay until his coffin was made. The cooling board was like an ironing board, only it had four sturdy legs.

They put a suit of clothes on him, what looked like an old suit of Massa's.

After the slaves came in from the fields that night we held his funeral. They dug a grave in the slave graveyard, which was different than the regular one behind the church. Some white folks came to the funeral. We sang "Hark from the Tomb" and "Amazing Grace," and Mama cried something fierce. All the children cried.

I heard Massa say in a low voice to Big Red, "Damn, I lost a prime nigra. Worth from three to five thousand."

ROBERT AND SOME of his friends had gone possum hunting. Robert missed the hunting he used to do at home and so Massa let him go. Grandma Sarry said if he fetched in five or six she'd cook them up just as Robert liked them, sprinkled with butter and pepper and baked down till the gravy was thick and brown. Robert liked to gnaw the bones.

Tonight, Grandma Sarry promised, she would make up a whole mess of possum for Robert and his friends.

MASSA LET THEM have the dogs. Robert knew how to tote possum home: split a stick and run their tail through the crack, then carry the stick across your shoulders. That way you didn't get bit. Sacks are no good. They gnaw their way out of sacks.

I was out in the quarters awaiting Robert's return when Mama called me into the house. I hated going inside because the June air was so soft and sweet. The baby was sleeping, so I thought I'd be free for a while.

Mistress had had her baby, a girl named Elizabeth Margaret, in May, the sweetest little baby girl with a beautiful little mouth and nose and fingernails like a real lady's. And true to Mistress's word, I was the baby's private nurse. I would belong to her, Mistress had explained, all of my life. I was the Burwells' gift to little Elizabeth Margaret.

Of course, that meant moving out of Mama's cabin and into the big house. I slept on a straw pallet on the floor next to the baby's cradle all night in case she cried. And cry she did, every two hours at first, and I was to run and get Ellie, the wet nurse brought up from the quarters to feed and change her. I was not to wake Mistress, and I was not to pick the baby up.

I did my chores well that first month. All day I kept the flies off little Elizabeth Margaret's face. I sang to her when she was awake, all the slave songs I knew. And I didn't even cry, though I missed my own bed, my own Mama next to me at night. I was still just five years old.

I WENT INTO the house. Sure enough little Elizabeth was crying. I went to look for Ellie, the wet nurse, but she was nowhere to be found. So I went back into the baby's room and did what I was told to do when she fussed. I rocked the cradle.

I reckon I rocked it too much because it tipped over and little Elizabeth Margaret fell out. There she was on the floor, crying as if Raw Head and Bloody Bones were both coming to get her. Well now, I was in a fix all right. I ran out into the hall and called out. I looked over the banister, but nobody was in sight. I could hear them sure enough, from the dining room, where they were eating and laughing.

I ran back into the baby's room. All I wanted to do was stop her from crying.

It was then that I saw the fireplace shovel, sitting there bold as the brass it was. In a wink I knew what to do. And so I grabbed the shovel and tried to pick up little Elizabeth Margaret with it, just like I'd seen servants do with ashes. Could she be heavier than a shovelful of ashes?

I tried and tried, but no matter. That no-count shovel wouldn't pick her up.

"Lizzy, what are you doing?"

Sure enough they came running then. A whole passel of them. The room was full of people of a sudden. People who had been nowhere on God's earth a few minutes ago. My mama, Ellie, the wet nurse, Mistress, even Massa.

Someone grabbed my hand and pulled the shovel out of it. Someone else picked up Elizabeth Margaret who wouldn't stop wailing if Moses himself came into the room. Someone grabbed my arm and handed me over to Ellie. It was Mistress. "Take this child outside and have her whipped good," Mistress said.

I was handed over from one person to another like a piece of meat on its way to the smokehouse. With each person who roughly grabbed me I grew in years. I was no longer five years old. I was every slave on Massa's plantation who'd ever been dragged to a tree to be tied up. I felt the choking fear, the numbing disbelief, the animal instinct to escape.

I felt like a possum treed by dogs.

I knew now why Uncle Raymond had hanged himself, even thinking such was going to happen to him. I recollect screaming, "Mama, help me. Massa, no, it's me, your little Lizzy." I screamed all their names while I felt myself thrust out the door and handed over to a grinning Big Red.

"Finally gonna get your comeuppance, ain't you, little gal?"

He had something to say with every action he took. Dragging me across the portico. "Think you're so special, do you?"

Tying me around the post of the portico. "I'll show you special. Sashaying around here with your nose in the air."

Delivering the first blow. "'Bout time Massa decided to break you."

I screamed until there wasn't any more voice left in me. He wasn't supposed to brand me with a hot iron, was he? Then why did it feel like a hot iron?

I screamed all their names. "Mama!" Where was she? Where was Grandma Sarry? Massa? Robert?

But the only one besides me who was on the place was Big Red. Even God was gone.

I MUST HAVE FAINTED. They told me later that Big Red went easy on me because I was only five years old. I wondered what he would do if I was grown-up.

But I was grown-up after that. Couldn't they see? I'd grown years that evening. If grown-up meant that you no longer trusted anybody. If grown-up meant that you trusted, even less, the part of you that was white. If grown-up meant knowing how stupid you'd been, thinking you were part of the family.

And if grown-up meant you knew you had one person in the world you could believe in, at least. Yourself.

LATER ON THAT NIGHT, sleeping on my straw pallet on the floor, I overheard Massa and Mistress arguing.

"I won't have her watching Elizabeth Margaret anymore," Mistress said. "She's like all mixed-race women. Everybody knows they're bad breeders and bad nursemaids. They are heinous, cursed by the devil. Mulattoes are monsters. I won't have it."

He said something to her then, but I couldn't hear, this father of mine. But she quieted down. And they kept allowing me to be Elizabeth Margaret's nursemaid, heinous as I was.

I RECKON THEY decided I needed to see my daddy again because within two weeks' time Daddy came to Hampden-Sydney.

Before that, nobody said anything to console me about being whipped.

"You be a good girl from now on," was all Grandma

Sarry said. But she made me some special gingerbread that was better than any cake I ever ate.

Mama just looked at me. "You gotta learn to behave, baby, 'cause there ain't a thing I can do for you if you don't."

"I know," I said.

"Thank heaven your daddy wasn't here. Sure as heaven, he'd try to do something. Thank heaven he wasn't here. But Massa makin' it up to you now. He's gonna bring your daddy here."

I wouldn't go near Massa or Mistress. Even though they gave me the baby to take care of again.

I wouldn't look at Robert at all. He came into the kitchen and tried to talk to me. "Come on over here and sit on my lap, little one. Like you always used to do."

I shook my head, no, surprised at how easy hate came. Surprised at how hate gave you back your dignity and made them understand that you were a person. Still, given all that, Robert was the hardest one to hate after all.

GRANDMA SARRY PUT three chickens in a pot and made up a batch of locust beer. Locust beer was my daddy's favorite. So were Grandma's chickens.

Mama came into the kitchen singing. She was wearing a new calico dress. "We all is gonna celebrate tonight," she said. She was beaming. I never could recollect her beaming and singing at all. She went about downcast most of the time. Now it was as if a whole sky of stars had been given to her.

All because my daddy was coming to visit.

"What we got to celebrate?" Grandma teased.

Mama looked at me. "Massa gonna buy your daddy. Massa says he could use him here since Raymond died. Your daddy gonna take Raymond's place. Massa done fetched him."

My daddy could make bricks and he knew all about farm tools, too. I was struck with fear. "No, you can't let Massa do that."

"What's wrong with you, girl? Don't you want Daddy George here all the time with us?"

"Suppose he loses a harness," was all I could say.

"No, no, it ain't gonna be like that," Mama promised. "Don't you worry. Your daddy knows what he's about. He's worth his salt, don't you worry."

She went around singing all afternoon. I wanted my daddy here, sure 'nuf. But I didn't trust any of it. Or anybody.

"BABY." DADDY FOLDED me in his arms. "What devilment went on here? They beat you?"

"Yes. And Mama says if you were here, it wouldn't have happened."

He didn't answer. I waited, but no answer came. I was sorry, right off, that I'd said it. I could feel his sadness. And I knew my daddy wouldn't lie just to make me feel better.

He stayed. But I couldn't spend nights with him and Mama in their cabin because I was needed in the big house for Elizabeth Margaret.

And I missed a whole week of good times in the evening when work was done and they celebrated down in the quarters. It was just like corn-shucking time down there. Mama always had some good old baked meat on the fire and a pile of sweet 'taters in the ashes. There was plenty of cake and even some pulled-syrup candy. They drank locust beer and corn liquor. They danced far into the night.

When I complained that I was missing all the fun, Grandma Sarry told me, "You got the rest of your life to be with your daddy 'cause he gonna be here all the time now."

It was Massa who stepped in and said I should have a day off to spend with my daddy. That surprised me. And what surprised me more was how solemn he was when he said it.

I spent the day with Daddy down at Dry Fork Creek. Grandma Sarry packed up some cold chicken and sweet 'taters and Daddy brought a jug of locust beer. We caught catfish and perch and a heap of suckers on that warm June day. And later on Grandma Sarry cooked the fish and collard greens in the kitchen of the big house just for me and Mama and Daddy.

It was almost good. If I pretended, I could forget Massa had me whipped. And there was Mama happier than a coon dog on a hunt because Daddy was here to stay.

BUT IT WAS NOT TO BE. And that night, I found out why Massa had been so solemn. He came into the kitchen and read us a letter. It said that he couldn't buy Daddy because Daddy's own master was moving to Tennessee and needed him. My daddy was not for sale.

We were all struck dumb as jackasses in the rain. Mama burst into tears and ran from the room. Daddy couldn't speak.

"I'm sorry, George," Massa said. Then he, too, walked out.

"Where is this Tennessee?" I asked Daddy.

"It's south, baby."

South was bad. All the slaves knew it. The farther south you went, the worse your lot became. They beat you regular-like and worked you till you died down South.

Daddy knelt in front of me. He put a hand on each of my shoulders. "You listen to me, little Lizzy," he said. "The only thing that works out is what you do for yourself."

I nodded yes.

"And I'm doin' for myself. My massa let me hire myself out as a brickmaker. Some of the money goes to him and some I get to keep for myself. I needs one hundred and twenty dollars a year to buy myself. When I get enough I'll buy myself, all right. And I'll come back here to this Virginny and get my family. I promise."

I said nothing.

"You believe me, Lizzy?"

"Yes."

But I didn't. And I knew for sure that I'd never see him again.

"Learn your book, Lizzy," he told me. "Get good at something. Then buy yourself. It's the only way."

That I believed.

DADDY GEORGE'S MASSA came to fetch him at the end of the week, and there were some blue devil minutes there when we had to tell him good-bye.

Mama couldn't stop crying as we watched his massa's wagon taking him away. I was still a little tyke then, but I understood my sorrow could not match my mama's. Grandma had to drag her back into the house and into the kitchen to dim her sobs, lest they anger Massa and Mistress.

Grandma spent the night with her in her cabin, and said she cried all night long. Next day when Mama came up to the big house to care for Mistress's younger children, I could see how cast down she was. She didn't talk to me, she didn't talk to the children who loved her, too. All my life I'd had to share her love with those children. And at times she was more of a mother to them than she was to me.

To make matters worse, Massa started to shower Mama with kindness to make up for the badness, like he always did. He sent special middlin's of meat to Grandma Sarry to cook for her and Mama and me. In the kitchen, Aunt

Charlotte's girls, who were overworked anyway, got jealous and went to Mistress, who got more jealous.

Mistress never could forget, you see, how I came to be in this world, and what Mama had to do with it.

We were in the kitchen, just about to sit down to eat that special middlin' of meat, when Mistress came in, her hair all askew, tearstains on her face.

"I want you to stop putting on airs," she told Mama. "Your husband is not the only slave that has been sold from this family. And you are not the only ones who have had to part. There are plenty more men about here if you want to be married. Just find yourself another one. You found my husband fast enough."

My mouth fell open so wide bees could build a honeycomb inside. Before Mama could even think of answering, Mistress walked out.

THAT WAS THE END of my childhood for me, if it didn't end when they whipped me. The years went on. Mama didn't marry. But the years took their pieces of the Burwell family, too.

Robert graduated from Hampden-Sydney and became a prig of a Presbyterian minister. John and Armistead graduated, too, and went out on their own. Benjamin was still in college. Anne married Hugh Garland, another prig, a Hampden-Sydney professor of Greek. Home yet were Mary, who would soon marry Hugh's brother; Fanny, who was sixteen; Charles, thirteen; William, eleven; and Elizabeth Margaret, now nine.

Since Elizabeth Margaret no longer needed a nurse-maid, I went back to attending her mother. She did not like me, I know, but the only reason for that was because her husband was my real father. What kept me safe was that I never let on that I knew it, never acted upon it, never played one against the other. I could have, I knew. Other children in my position did. But I decided I'd rather take her orders, her coldness, than go work in the fields like other girls of fourteen. Like Jane. Never would I be made to eat worms. I'd die first.

I WAS FOURTEEN and I knew I was pretty. I knew it because Mama worried, because she tied my hair back in braids and always put a fresh white kerchief around the neckline of my dress so my bosoms wouldn't show. "You gotta be careful," she told me. "I wasn't much older when I had you. And it weren't my idea, Lizzy, believe me."

It was the first and only time she'd said anything about it to me. But I said nothing. I knew when to keep a still tongue in my head.

But I didn't really know how pretty I was until Eleanor, daughter of Reverend Paxton, asked me to be a bridesmaid in her wedding.

"You can make your own gown," she said. "You sew so beautifully. I have Mr. Burwell's permission to ask you. The gowns will be pink silk. The other bridesmaid's dresses are coming in from Petersburg. You can copy them."

"Oh, Eleanor, I don't know what to say."

"Say yes, Lizzy. You'll be the prettiest one I have."

"But what will people say?"

"You mean because you're mulatto? They won't say anything. They know my father freed his slaves and sent them to Liberia. They know what my family's beliefs are and they respect them."

And so I said yes. Mama had kept me at my sewing in the last nine years, so I'd graduated to making aprons and shifts and even a dress or two for myself. I knew I could do it. Mama said I had a special gift for sewing. I worked hard on that dress. I stayed up nights because Mistress wouldn't give me time during the days. She didn't like my being in that wedding. I heard her tell Massa so. But he won that argument.

Finally, two days before the wedding, I finished the bodice and the sleeves. I really wanted to be in that wedding. Just having Eleanor ask me to make my dress showed me that people knew what I could do. Of course I was flattered, and I wanted to show everybody not only the dress but me. How I had grown. How pretty I was.

I shall never forget it. The other bridesmaids and all of Eleanor's family praised my work and appearance. Everyone was nice to me. It was the first time I felt like a person since I was whipped, since Daddy had been taken from us.

Only one thing happened to ruin it. And it came from the most unexpected person. It came from Robert.

I was standing around sipping punch at the reception when Robert came up to me with a girl on his arm. "This is Anna," he said.

And then, "Anna, this is Lizzy, our slave girl. Don't let the dress and all the fuss over her fool you."

I stammered hello. Tears came to my eyes. But I held my head high.

"Curtsy," Robert ordered.

I understood then. Anna was not so pretty. She must be bowed to. I curtsied.

Later, when he was alone, Robert came up to me again.

"You didn't have to introduce me that way," I stammered.

"Yes, I did, Lizzy. You're getting too filled up with yourself. Too uppity. I did it for your own good. You don't want some master having to break you someday."

My heart fell. This from Robert? I knew he tended to be a prig, but when had this happened to him? What had they taught him in the seminary?

I chided myself. I'd vowed to hate him once, after I'd been whipped. I'd vowed to trust no white person who was for slavery. But I supposed I'd never given up on Robert. He was my most difficult lesson, still not learned. But sadly, to be learned in the future.

ROBERT MARRIED HIS ANNA soon after. Her real name was Margaret Anna Robertson from Petersburg. I was not in the wedding. I did not expect to be, did not want to be. But a month before, Robert came to me.

"Anna liked the dress you made for yourself for Eleanor's wedding," he said coldly. "Since money is a consideration, she would like you to make her bridesmaids' dresses. There will be two of them."

"I don't have time," I told him. "I have my chores. Your mama gave me no time to make my own dress. I had to work at night."

"Are you saying no to me, Lizzy?"

I did not answer.

"Never say no to your master," he reminded me.

"You're not my master," I told him. "You're my half brother."

I knew it was cheeky. I'd bantered with Robert in the past many times. Now I was pushing to see how far I could go.

He remained becalmed, but I saw his blue eyes go icy. "You've been given too many privileges," he said flatly. "I'm going to have to see that that changes."

I stared at him. What did that mean?

"Hasn't my father told you?"

I felt a numbness in my bones. "No."

"From here on in, I am your master. You're to come and live with me and Anna. Now I want those two dresses made. I'll handle my mother. And you're to come with us to Petersburg for the wedding, where you will attend Anna as she deserves to be attended. As your mistress. You'll fetch and serve for the both of us from now on."

IT WAS ALL TRUE. Massa informed me later that day. He had given me to Robert as a wedding gift.

"It's best all around, Lizzy," he said. "You're growing up. What will you do here? Think of me. It's getting too complicated for me to have my beautiful mixed-race daughter around anymore. My wife won't be kind to you in the future. Who will you marry around here? A field hand? I just don't know what to do with you. Robert will. He's a minister."

It was the first time in my life he ever called me his daughter. Was this supposed to make me feel better? It didn't.

US SLAVES ALWAYS knew one truth. To be a slave was horrible. But to be a slave in a family without means or money was worse. It was lowering yourself. Every slave wanted to work for quality people. Robert was quality, to be sure, and so was Anna, but one soon learned that without money, quality got shoved in the background.

The name of the town was Ellerslie. It was in Virginia. Robert was pastor of the little local church. It was a coal mining town, as miserable as a place could be.

I was the only servant. And I soon learned that what had been done by three servants back home was all to be done by me. We settled in. I cooked and dusted and in a few hours the coal dust was back again, on everything. I washed clothes and dusted. I swept, scoured, milked the cow, and tried to keep the dust out of the milk. I kept the poultry fed and brushed the coal dust from the horses' coats. I attended Anna, brushed her hair, and dusted. I waited on Robert, and brushed the coal dust off his good frock coat.

Although she had already worked out in the world as a teacher, Anna was spoiled. She talked all the time about how she was descended from the Spotswoods, like I was expected to know who they were, or care. Her parents had died, she'd gone to live with an uncle, and he, too, died. She'd gone out teaching. But her parents once had money, and like everyone who'd once had money, she never let you forget it.

She became hysterical over trifles, she got bad head-aches, and she was either flying up there with the angels or cast down with her own blue devils. I was expected to know the mood and work with it.

I'd say she needed a good serving of marrow from the jowl of a hog, that woman.

Did Robert love her? Who knew anything about Robert these days. We never talked except when he gave me orders, and those he expected to be followed quickly and without replies. He was all the time out of the house making his pastor calls, and when he was home he locked himself away, writing his sermons. To bother him you had to be the archangel Michael knocking at the door.

We stayed in that place for three years, during which Anna had two children, Mary and John. Carrying the children she was impossible, hysterical and crying most of the time. After they were born she drove me daft having me check on them every half hour lest they smother in their cribs. She courted disaster, that woman. She waited for it. Sometimes at night I heard her crying in their room and heard Robert trying to comfort her. These times I almost felt sorry for him.

Then finally, when Robert couldn't stand the coal dust anymore, when Anna said she didn't want her children breathing it in, he got another job and we moved.

I was almost eighteen and worn to the bone. Now, besides all my household chores, I was caring for two children. And Anna was in a childbearing way again. We moved to Hillsborough, in North Carolina.

ANNA WAS NOT STUPID. She could recite *Paradise Lost* by heart. But she did not know how to find Robert again after she lost him in the coal town of Ellerslie.

And that's what she had done. Lost him as sure as I'd lost my Daddy George. Only Robert was there, in front of her. They bumped into each other. They were expecting another child. But they scarce spoke to each other unless she complained to him about how bad she was feeling, about the other children, about me and what a vexation I was to her.

HILLSBOROUGH WAS MORE to Robert's liking. He made more money, four hundred dollars a year. It was a lovely little town full of busy, happy people, all slaveholders, twelve miles west of Durham, North Carolina, which was the seat of something or other. The county, I think, though I never understood why a county needed a seat to sit down on. There were also some free nigra people, the likes of whom I had never seen before, who went about being in business for themselves, being barbers and craftsmen and farmers.

Anna and Robert moved into a two-story frame house, with big windows and two rooms on each floor, not counting the kitchen. It was surrounded by lovely trees and on top of a hill. Anna had a greenhouse. She had roses and all kinds of flowers. She had a meadow and a vegetable garden for which she got all kinds of compliments, though I did all the work. She had a swing and a white picket fence. And you could walk to town.

The town was full of doctors and lawyers and genteel, professional-quality people.

"You'll love it," Robert told her. "You'll love being the parson's wife there."

Anna hated it. She called it a mudhole. But then Anna hated everything in those days. Especially me.

FOR SOME REASON, that first year in Hillsborough, despite her husband's happiness, or mayhap because of it, Anna was determined to wreak vengeance upon me.

She blamed me for everything. For the rain when there was too much and the muddy water that came into the well so we couldn't do the washing. For the sun when it beat down on the quiet, sleepy streets.

We had another slave woman in the house, name of Mary Ann. She was the cook, so I didn't have those duties, thank heaven. Mary Ann was sure of herself but never cocky. She was proud of herself yet never arrogant. One day when she heard me and Anna arguing, she took me aside.

"Doan know who brung you up," she said, "but girl, didn't you ever learn the first rule of livin' with a woman like that?"

I shook my head no.

"Got one mind for the boss to see, got another for what I know is me," she quoted.

But I never could keep my anger private and put on a smiling face, as I was supposed to do. And worst of all, I never learned to humble myself to Anna's liking.

Robert let Anna rule the house, which was the problem. No matter what she decided, it was all right. Indeed, if she went to him for advice, all he would say was, "I don't know, figure it out yourself. I've my own work to do."

So Anna was left on her own to figure, to plot, to plan her sneak attacks on me. And she was like a fox in the henhouse. Still, she would bother Robert with stupid questions like, "Why does the egg man call me the Widow Burwell?"

I knew why. It was because Anna was the only one who went to the door to deal with the egg man, the milkman, the man who delivered our chickens. They never saw Robert, though they sure knew of his existence. They went to his church on Sunday. Still they called her the Widow Burwell and flirted with her. And to her shame she flirted back.

Robert spent his time being a minister. He preached twice on Sunday. He visited his people. He held Bible classes. Everyone thought him warm and generous, handsome and likely, holy and studious, and of quality. He never told any of them, "I don't know."

———

ANNA HAD JUST HAD her third baby, a girl, and was more moody and sad than ever. Though I am ashamed to admit it, we came to blows one day over a shell and wax wreath. To make extra money, she made and sold shell and wax flowers and wreaths.

One day she'd made a particularly lovely wreath and, as always, I was helping her to carry her flowers to church for sale. As always, she was fussing at me. I had a headache that morning, I recollect. I didn't feel well and I was in no mood for her Brer Fox, Brer Rabbit games.

I was afraid I was getting cholera. An epidemic was going around Orange County that spring. Two children had already died of it.

I longed for Grandma Sarry, for a serving of her corn pone soaked with peas and pot likker. For a slice of her side meat. Mary Ann could not cook like Grandma Sarry to save her soul. That morning I even would have welcomed a dose of wild cherry and poplar leaves mixed with black haw and slippery elm leaves. In other words, a dose of the bitters.

I suppose I wasn't the only one with the miseries that morning. I'd just brought Robert a cup of coffee in his study where he was practicing his sermon about sorrow and guilt, fear, sickness, and evil.

I dropped her lovely shell and wax wreath and it broke into pieces on the floor. Anna screamed and jumped on me like a frog on a lily pad. "You are a constant vexation to me. You are the cross in my life, the thorn in my side."

She shouted it, attacking me with slaps and blows about my head and face. What could I do? I had to defend myself. I couldn't let anyone treat me like that. I struck her back. My hand caught at the side of her face, leaving a red mark. I stepped back, horrified at what I had done.

"You dare!" she shouted. "You dare strike me? Mary Ann! Mary Ann!" She called out to the only other woman in the house. And Mary Ann came running.

"You two fussing again?" she asked.

"It's more than fussing," Anna told her. "She struck me. She attacked me in my own house. Go and get my husband, Mary Ann. Go and get Master Robert.

In later years, when God gave me wisdom, I would know that Robert was simply a man caught between his wife and his half sister. That day I saw none of it. I only saw Robert standing in front of me in his study. Furious.

In his hand he had a newspaper. And he pointed to an advertisement for a runaway slave named Betty.

He read it. "I burnt her with a hot iron on the left side of her face," the ad read. "I did it to break her. If you see her, you'll know her by this mark."

Robert shook the newspaper at me. "Do you see what some masters do?"

I did not answer.

"I am not a cruel man, Lizzy, but you must be taught a lesson. You must learn to acknowledge that Anna is your mistress. I cannot think what to do with you, so I am going to hire you out next door, to Mr. Bingham. You will do chores there and then come here. You will work between the two houses. Do you understand?"

I understood. Bingham was a nigra hater. He was a hard, cruel man who walked backward going to and from the school where he was principal, for fear a nigra might creep up behind him and knock him in the head.

He thrashed his students all the time. Everyone knew that he carried a pistol. He was on the local patrol to protect white citizens from a possible slave rebellion. After a man named Nat Turner conducted an uprising in 1831, many white people feared slave rebellions.

He was also known as a slave breaker. People sent their slaves to him to be broken, people like Robert, who were too genteel to do it themselves.

"I don't want to go there, Robert," I said, "please."

He paid me no never mind. And that night I reported to the back door of Mr. William J. Bingham, principal of Hillsborough Academy and local breaker of slaves.

IT ALL BEGAN proper-like. Mr. Bingham acted like a parson himself at first. His wife was a quiet, mousy woman who couldn't come up with an opinion if Moses himself asked her to. She treated her husband like her master. When I got to know him, I understood why. She had long since given up trying to be a person in her own right. If I had any smarts, I'd have taken lessons from her.

I was to stay at their place nights since they had a six-month-old baby who needed constant attention and cried a lot. The baby woke, fussing, at six in the morning. I got up then and carried it to its mother for nursing. Then I cleaned all the fireplaces and started fires in them. At eight we had prayers. I was to soon learn that he was the prayingest man I ever was to meet, that Mr. Bingham. I suppose he had a lot to pray about and make up for.

After prayers I served breakfast. I didn't have to cook, thank heaven. They had a cook, name of Jenny. After breakfast I cleaned up.

When Mr. Bingham left, I was to stand in the front

hallway and hand him his hat and coat and say, "Have a good day, sir."

It was something he was persnickety about, and I was corrected many times before he allowed that I did 't just right.

After he left I was to go home, next door, just in time to dress and feed the Burwell children. At home I cleaned up, I cared for the children, I mended and sewed, and I was at Anna's beck and call all day. Then it was back to the Binghams in time to serve supper and clean up and put the baby to bed.

I ran back and forth between the two houses like a chicken with its head cut off, for two weeks, until I was worn down in body and spirit. I slept when I could and ate when I could and didn't mouth off at anybody. I was too scared to.

ALL THE WHILE I felt Mr. Bingham watching me when I wasn't looking. He watched me all the time, that man, and it gave me the blue devils. I thought, if ever a man scared me like Raw Head or Bloody Bones of my childhood, it was him. He could pray all he wanted to and make me kneel when he prayed, but he was still evil, that man. I saw it in his small beady eyes and in the way he held his half-bald head. He all the time looked like he had the stomach miseries. Like he needed a good dose of scurvy-grass tea.

He was plotting something. That's what I saw when his evil eyes looked at me. Turned out I was right, too.

One evening when I'd been there two weeks and was putting the baby to bed, he stood outside the nursery door.

"Come to my study as soon as you're finished here," he ordered.

I felt like I had a cold in my bones. If I could have run, I would have, but this man always wore his pistol, even in the house. I had no doubt that he'd shoot me if I ran. Besides, before I even came here Robert had warned me, "Remember, in North Carolina a master cannot be charged with battery against a slave."

In his study, Mr. Bingham closed the door and got right to it. "Take off your dress, I am going to whip you."

I drew myself up proudly. "No, Mr. Bingham, I shall not take off my dress before you. And you won't whip me unless you prove the stronger."

I knew that much. I'd die first. But he grabbed a rope and tried to tie my hands. We fought. I tried to force him away, but he was the stronger.

He ripped my dress from my back, and with a piece of rawhide began to flog me. Oh God, I can still feel the torture now, the terrible, excruciating agony of those moments. But I wouldn't cry out. I wouldn't give him the satisfaction.

He finally finished with his devil's work and I wrapped my dress around me the best I could and dragged myself out of the house and home.

There I found Robert and Anna, quietly enjoying their evening before the fire in the parlor. I stumbled in, bleeding and holding my dress about me.

I stood in front of Robert, who was reading. He did not look up at me. "Why did you let Bingham flog me?" I demanded.

Still, he wouldn't look at me. Nor would Anna, who just sat there making her shell flowers.

"I did everything that was expected of me. I gave no mouth. I did no foolishment. Why?"

"Go away," Robert said.

"No, I won't. I deserve an answer. You sent me there for this, didn't you? You wanted it for me. You know he's a slave breaker."

"Go away, Lizzy."

"Well, I'm not broken. Nobody can break me."

He put his book down. He stood up. He picked up his wooden chair and threw it at me. I ducked, but it grazed the side of my face and knocked me down

"Go away or you'll be sorry." He stood looking down at me.

I struggled to my feet and left. But I did not go back to the Binghams until the next morning.

I CRIED MYSELF to sleep. You would think Anna would come and offer me something for my bleeding back, but she didn't. I knew what I needed. A bath with soaking mullein leaves. Tea made of peach-tree leaves. But I had nothing, nobody.

THE NEXT MORNING my back hurt precious bad, but I was becalmed. I served breakfast to Anna and Robert. I know I would have forgiven him if he gave me one kind word, I needed kindness so badly. But he gave me nothing.

I went back to Bingham's and acted with dignity.

A week went by and the next Friday he came at me again.

Again I fought him. He had a new rope and a new rawhide whip. This time I bit his finger. He grabbed up a stick and beat me with it, but again I wouldn't cry out. He beat me about the head and shoulders and back until I was again bleeding.

Then something happened. He stood there as I cowered in front of him, warding off more blows. He was breathing heavily, exhausted.

Then, of a sudden, he started to cry.

"It would be a sin to beat you anymore," he said. "I'll never beat you again, Lizzy. I promise."

ANNA TOOK UP AGAIN where Bingham left off. No longer did I have to work for him. Just as he turned kind, I was summoned home by Robert to take up all my old chores in full.

Anna was holding her new little girl, Ann, when she came at me for failing to keep up the fire in the parlor. "I know what happened between you and Bingham," she told me. "He came the other day to talk with Robert. After all, Robert is his pastor."

She glared at me. "So, you think we lost."

"I think nothing, ma'am."

"You'll be more of a vexation now to me than ever."

We argued. She pushed me into sassiness. Robert came into the room then with a broom handle in his hands.

"I'll not have any more of this. Stop it, the both of you!"

"She sassed me, Robert. You have to do something.

Bingham couldn't. She made that man cry. You must do it. You are her master. Your power is absolute."

What did she mean by *absolute*? I feared the worst.

It came about then. Robert came at me with the broomstick. He beat me about the head and shoulders until my head rang with the pain of it. I struggled. I fought him just as I'd fought Bingham.

I felt blood streaming down the side of my face. It was like being attacked by a possum. I felt removed, as if I were somewhere far away when I heard Anna yelling, "No, no, Robert. No more please, you'll kill her."

She kept saying it, and he kept right at me. I fell to the floor, and it was then that I saw Anna kneeling at Robert's side, baby in arms, begging him to stop.

The baby was screaming. I worried about the baby. And this is the house of a parson, I thought crazily, while pain shot through my shoulders and arms and back.

"I'll subdue her proud, rebellious spirit once and for all," Robert was saying to Anna.

She clutched at his arm. "Think, think of what you are doing to yourself. You're a man of God, Robert."

That made him stop like somebody had thrown cold water at him. Her words struck him right in the face. He stood, stunned. He ran his hand across his forehead. He looked at his hands. They were trembling. He threw down the broomstick and stared down at me as if he had no more sense than a hooty owl.

"Dear God, what have I done?"

I was on the floor. I couldn't move. I was sure my left arm was broken. My face was bleeding, and I felt as if my head was split open. Lights flashed in front of my eyes, and then for a moment or two I couldn't see at all.

The baby was hiccuping, the fire crackling, and for a moment they seemed like the only sounds in the world.

Robert knelt down beside me. "Get up, Lizzy."

"I don't know if I can."

"You can. I'll help you." And so he did. Then he took the baby from Anna's arms and directed her. "Go with her and bandage her up. Put her arm in a sling if you have to. Let me know if I should call a doctor."

He was babbling, then of a sudden he stopped and looked at me. "Lizzy, Lizzy," he said. "I promise I will never strike you another blow again."

Robert and Anna had always needed money, but now, with a fourth child coming, they needed it like a coon dog needed to hunt. To that end they started their school. An advertisement in the paper listed the cost: English studies, $17.50, French, $15.00, Music, $25.00, Drawing and Painting, $10.00, and Sewing as for a Fine Lady, $25.00.

The sewing was taught by me.

They called it Burwell's Female Academy. What the ad didn't say was that the young ladies would also be making their own beds, helping to wash their own dishes, and doing their own mending. Anna wouldn't lay herself low enough to do such tasks. And all the help they had was the cook and me.

The school was a success, which had a lot to do with Robert teaching, too. That, and the Presbyterian Session and the Ladies' Benevolent Society giving money to make the house bigger.

But best of all, Anna and Robert were working together and had too much to do to fuss at me anymore. Anna

didn't even fuss when I was asked to be in six weddings between October of 1837 and April of 1838. Of course, I was
to make my own gowns, and I was surprised as a hooty owl
caught in daylight when Robert offered to buy the fabric.

"You'll be a walking advertisement for our school, Lizzy,"
he told me. "I can't afford not to."

Two of the weddings, that of Miss Ann Nash and Miss
Susan Atwell, were held around Christmas, and so the occasions were twice as festive.

But a different dress for each one! I wrote to my mother,
thinking she could make one dress for me for a spring wedding. "Please, could you make me a pretty frock?" I wrote.
"I can send the fabric and the pattern."

I'd written to my mother faithfully over the years, but
she never wrote back. This time she did.

"Just make sure you don't appear too likely to those
white mens at the weddings," she wrote. "Or you'll end up
with child, like I did."

That was all. A brutal reply. I hid my disappointment.
I made the dress myself.

I LONGED TO GET AWAY. The house was full to the brim
with chilluns. The students, whose ages were from ten to
fourteen, were all just chilluns after all and they needed
fussing over. They needed to have their spirits raised up
when they got homesick. There was lots of crying at night
when the lights went out.

One girl, fourteen-year-old Susan Murphy, cried every
night. It was my job to sit and soothe her because, as
Robert said, "You have had your lessons in sorrow."

"I can't stay here any longer," Susan sobbed in her bed. "I want to go home. If my father doesn't send the stage for me, I'll walk."

I talked to her. I comforted her. I told her how I would never see my father again, how I'd been sent away from my mother at fourteen.

She listened as if to a fairy tale. *That's what my life is,* I told myself. *A fairy tale in which the witches and the dragons always win.*

I didn't sleep myself that night. I yearned to escape from that place. I'd met many other house slaves by now in Hillsborough. And they all went about a lot more free than I was. More than that, I'd met free nigra women who made their own living as storekeepers, midwives, tavern keepers, or owners of cook shops.

I knew for certain that someday I wanted to buy my own freedom as my father and Grandma Sarry had said. But for now, all I wanted, all I needed, was to get away from that house.

THAT'S WHERE I ran into trouble. Just like Brer Rabbit in the briar patch. Wanting to get away and do on my own. Wanting to get away from that house full of noisy little girls always up to some devilment, who all learned, straight-away, that I was the one to go to for help and comfort. Those little girls who didn't know a thing about hoeing a row of cotton, or eating the heads off worms, or waiting on a table, or sleeping on a pallet on the floor next to a cranky baby.

When my chance came to get away, I jumped on it like

a coon dog picking up scent. I didn't think twice. I minded that it was sent to me by God.

My CHANCE CAME when I was a bridesmaid at the wedding of Miss Jane Pitwell to Master John Dillard in March of 1838. As always, I'd made my own dress. It was yellow organza with a neckline that showed plenty of my bosoms and with no white neck scarf to hide anything.

I was all of twenty years old and ready to break away from the harness. And when Mr. Alexander Kirkland from Ayr Mount Plantation saw me in that dress, he had a crack in his voice.

"You made it yourself?"

He was over six feet tall and had what the white folk called "a commanding presence." Always I'd wondered what that meant. Now I knew.

"Yes," I said. "I do all my own clothes. And those of Mistress Burwell, too. I also teach sewing at the school."

"I wish you could teach it to my wife and niece Catherine," he said. Was he just a bit in his cups? He looked as if he'd had a quart of locust beer.

But my, he was handsome. And the way he spoke to me, like an equal, was a caution. I liked that. "You'd have to ask Master Robert," I said.

"I'd pay you."

"You'd have to pay him."

"Hires you out, does he?"

I thought of Bingham. "Sometimes."

"What's your name, then?"

"Lizzy. Lizzy Hobbs."

"Well, Lizzy Hobbs, would you dance with me?"

I stopped right there, like a jackass in front of a fence. I did have some sense. And I'd made a rule for myself. Never dance with a white man at a wedding. No sense in stirring up trouble.

The upshot of it all was that Mr. Alex Kirkland, thirty-three years on God's good earth and without the sense of a grasshopper, asked Master Robert could he hire me out so's I could teach his wife and his niece to sew.

Mr. Alex Kirkland of Ayr Mount, a mile east of town, who, as a cadet at a military academy in Connecticut, had been dismissed for hitting another cadet. Who was rumored to beat his wife. Who had once shot and killed a man in a hunting accident and sold two of his slaves to the local slave dealer because they were unruly and insolent.

He had one baby son. He had a merchandising business in town. His man drove him to and from town every day in his fancy carriage.

He could fetch me in that carriage, he told Robert. He would pay Robert well.

"Do you know what a treasure you have in her?" I overheard him asking Robert.

And Robert, who knew his treasure could bring him needed money, mumbled something about always knowing. And how would Mr. Kirkland treat me, he wanted to know. There was to be no physical abuse. After all, he'd heard things.

"All talk," Mr. Kirkland said. "You know how people in

this small town like to talk." And so Mr. Alex Kirkland, whose wife was then expecting her second child, promised no. He would not abuse me.

AYR MOUNT WAS on a hill outside of town right next to the Jones place. It was more of a big farm than a plantation, but I suppose it deserved the fancified name. It had slave cabins, little nigra chilluns running about the yard, the whole cloth of a plantation. The victuals were good, too. He had a cook name of Rainy, who was all the time feeding everybody. He had house girls named Peg and Joy, a butler who also drove the carriage, name of Arnold, and a passel of slaves in the fields whose names I never did get to know. He also had a granny woman, name of Parthena, whose onliest job was to look after little colored chilluns.

Mr. Alexander growed everything to feed and clothe his people on that plantation, except coffee and sugar and salt. It was a right pretty place, about a hundred acres. He had sheep, too, and they used the wool for winter clothes, and some of the slaves weaved cloth all day long.

If I seem to take on about the place it's because it was so lovely, like a dream come true for me at first. His wife, another Anna, was as different from Robert's Anna as the sun was from the moon. She was the sweetest thing this side of freedom.

Two days a week Mr. Kirkland fetched me "home" from Robert's place.

At Ayr Mount I would take tea with his wife and his ten-year-old niece who lived with them. I was also invited to dine at the supper table.

"Like a tutor from my childhood," Mr. Kirkland said. "You didn't make the tutor dine alone in the kitchen."

At first I was powerful scared about dining with white people. But I'd served at enough tables to know what to do and what not to do. And so I was accepted as one of them.

There was a problem though, and it was as sticky as a crock of spilled molasses. I couldn't make friends with Peg and Joy, no matter how I tried.

"You got yourself so turned around," Peg told me, "your head is on backwards. You ain't nigra anymore and you sure ain't white, girl. You hafta decide what you wanna be."

Indeed, what was I? It was a caution. And I was more confused than ever before in my life.

But I did what I was hired to do. I spent those two days a week teaching Anna Kirkland and her niece to sew. I showed them how to cut and fit, baste and stitch. In this case we had a difficult task. Mr. Kirkland wanted a white duster made of linen, made cutaway style, with long tails.

We worked on that coat until the cows came home and finished it in two weeks, and Mr. Kirkland allowed that it was as fine a coat as a man could want.

"You certainly are a treasure," he said.

How much of a treasure I was soon to find out.

I DON'T KNOW WHAT brought the devilment about. I never sashayed in front of that man. I never made eyes at him, and all the while I spent at Ayr Mount I dressed proper-like. No low necklines. And I always wore a neckerchief.

But in the fourth week of going to his house, he came at me. Like quality ladies all did, his wife and niece made afternoon calls, and he made sure they were out of the house, first. But always he made sure I had chores enough to keep me home. Then he sent Peg and Joy on some work down at the loom house. I was in the parlor, sewing, and when he came in he was in his cups, the smell of corn liquor on him, his eyes all glassy-like.

He came at me like a rutting hog, his hands all over me.

"Master Kirkland," I said, "please, sir."

"Please what?"

"Leave off."

"You telling me what to do? I'm the master around here, and I do as I please."

"But sir, it isn't right."

"You telling me what's right, you nigra you? You think because you sit at our table you're not still a slave? I hired you, girl, and you'll do as I say. This is part of the bargain. I don't care what Master Robert says. You're just chattel. You have no call to say no to me."

All the time he was unbuttoning my dress. I recollect, likely he's right. Likely I have no call to say no. I should do as he wishes.

I was supposed to give myself over to him because he was white and I was nigra. Because he was master and I was a slave. Just like my mama had done with Master Burwell.

Still, I fought him, as fierce as I'd fought Mr. Bingham. But this man was too strong for me. He slapped my face so's I near fainted. The blow sent me somewhere else, not here at all. So I succumbed. I remember screaming and him putting his filthy hand over my mouth. I recollect thinking: God is soon gonna kill this man if He's the God I know. And then I did faint, after all.

MR. ALEXANDER KIRKLAND made me bring myself to rights, made me stop crying. I remember he shoved a glass of whiskey at me to becalm me, but I'd never had whiskey so I near choked on it. He made me put on a new dress and sit at the supper table with them that evening.

"You behave," he said. "You tell anybody and I'll kill you. The authorities won't question me, not in this state. I mean it. You don't even tell Master Robert. I don't care if he is kin."

I was frightened as a hog going to slaughter, sitting at table with them that night. I couldn't eat. Master Kirkland coaxed me. Nicely.

"You don't eat you'll get sickly, Lizzy. I can't send you home to Robert ailing."

Somehow I ate. My head was aching. I told him I had a headache and he took pity on me and gave me laudanum.

I NEVER PRACTICED conjure, but I reverenced it too much not to hold some belief in it. As a child I'd seen it done in the quarters on Master Burwell's plantation many times. Grandma Sarry even did it on occasion. But only for good.

Could I do it? I vowed to try, so that night I went into the kitchen where Peg was preparing biscuit dough to make in the morning.

"What you want in here?" she asked. "Ain't you 'fraid you'll get dirty?"

"You got any nuts?"

"What kind?"

"Any kind will do. Walnuts, almonds."

She fetched some from a crock and eyed me. "They come dear," she said. "What you gonna do?"

I set one down on the wooden table and split it in half and put it in my apron pocket.

"Ain't you gonna eat it?" she asked.

I didn't answer.

Understanding lit up her eyes. "You conjure?" she asked.

"No."

"Why you split that nut then? I know what that means. My grandma used to conjure."

A new look in her eyes then. Respect. "Lord bless you. You still remembers who you are after all."

SURE 'NUF, NEXT MORNING he came to the breakfast table late, that man. And when he came, he had a splitting headache. His face looked like ashes from the fireplace. He looked old of a sudden. His eyes were sunken in.

"Coffee, Peg," he ordered. "Make sure it's hot. And get me my laudanum."

While she stood over his shoulder pouring the coffee out of the silver pot, Peg gave me a small smile.

He had the headache all day. I knew what he needed, jimsonweed beat up into a poultice and tied around his head. And another string tied around his head with the knot in front to draw out the pain. But I kept a still tongue in my head about it. Let him suffer.

He was so sick that Arnold the butler had to drive me home that day. And I didn't tell Robert what had happened. I kept my own counsel. Because I believed Alexander Kirkland really would kill me.

HE KEPT AT ME whenever the evil possessed him, that man. He had me whenever he wanted. I fought him every time, but it did no good.

Did Anna, his wife, suspect anything? I lived in terror that she would find out because she was so good to me. I didn't want her hurt in this sordid business, especially since she was carrying his second child.

Peg kept me supplied with nuts. And allst I could say is that he got migraine headaches of a sudden, and he had them all the time now.

He consulted with his doctor who gave him more laudanum. He took to drinking, regular-like. He lay on the couch in the parlor all day, half out of his senses. He stopped going to the store. He let his manager run it for him.

He got fat. He quit chewing tobacco. He became easily agitated and all the time talked about dying.

God punished him in other ways, too, ways that had nothing to do with me. Scarlet fever came to the quarters of Ayr Mount that summer. Bad. Three of his field hands died right off, and he had to have shanties built in a field for the other sick ones. They called it "shantytown," and food had to be carried there and left outside the shanties.

At night it looked like a scene from hell, that field with sticks of fat pine dipped in tar and burning, sticking out of the ground.

He lost seven field hands in all. I hoped it wasn't my doing. But I misdoubt I could do all that just by splitting nuts.

ALL THE WHILE he kept preying on me. He'd all the time follow me about the house and seize his moments when his wife and niece were out making calls. I didn't tell Robert. I wrote to my mother and never told her. She'd blame it on me. She'd say I was loose. What was worst of all was that if anybody did find out, I would be blamed. I, the nigra wench. The pretty nigra girl and the master of the house. It happened all the time. People expected it. It wouldn't be thought of as anything so terrible. Still, the blame would be mine.

Soon I was in a childbearing way and I panicked. What should I do? What would Robert and Anna say? I put off telling Robert as long as I could.

Finally I had to. And Robert's response was just what I expected. "You should have known better than to take up with that man, Lizzy. I'm disappointed in you."

"I didn't, Robert. He forced me. And he said he'd kill me if I told you."

For a moment he studied on that. Then, "You should have come to me. He's nothing but a drunken sot. His business is failing. He's stopped coming to church. I feel sorry for his wife."

"What am I going to do, Robert?"

"I'd send you home to Virginia, but my father has died and my mother is living with Anne and her husband, Hugh Garland. I can't burden them with this. Have your baby here, and then you go back when you and the child are ready to travel."

"Why can't I stay here?"

"Because I can't afford the gossip. People love to take on about something like this. I can't afford hurting the school."

There was some kind of a showdown between Robert and Master Kirkland. I don't know what happened, but money changed hands. Robert paid him. But he was to admit that the child was his if asked. So the reputation of Robert and the school wouldn't suffer.

My baby was born in midwinter of that year. Robert hired a doctor to attend me. "Pa would turn over in his grave if I did anything less," he said.

Did I mourn Master Burwell, my real father? For a few moments, yes, but having a child put the chill on that. I now knew what my mother had gone through, having me, submitting to him like I'd had to submit to Kirkland.

I named the baby boy George Pleasant Hobbs, not Kirkland. I named him after my Daddy George. Would Kirkland claim my son as one of his slaves? I worried that like a dog worried a bone, but Robert spoke to him about that, too, and assured me that I and the baby now belonged to his mother.

I went home with George Pleasant Hobbs when he was four months old, in April. Kirkland died soon after. People said he died from his drinking and his headaches, but I knew he died from the evil inside him. They say he cried out to the Lord for forgiveness before he died. On his tombstone is written this: "Gone where the wicked cease from troubling and the weary are at rest."

Elizabeth Keckley: From a Virginia Slave to the White House

W HEN LIZZY returned to Virginia early in 1842, she went to a farm that had a lovely view of the Appomattox River. She and her baby son were welcomed at the farm, called Mansfield. It had nearly three hundred acres of fields, numerous trees and barns, and a score of slaves.

It was owned by Anne and Hugh Garland. Anne was the oldest daughter of Lizzy's father and old master, Armistead Burwell.

Here Lizzy was reunited with her mother, Aggy, her aunt Charlotte, and her three cousins, Amy, Hanna, and Lucy. All of them, including Lizzy and her son George, belonged now to Mary Burwell, wife of Armistead.

If Lizzy ever knew happiness as a slave, it was in Virginia with the Garlands. She was a nursemaid and substitute mother to Anne Garland's toddlers, Nannie and Maggie.

But within two years, Hugh Garland, the breadwinner, was bankrupt. Financial times were bad all over. He had to leave Mansfield and take his family to Petersburg, a bustling manufacturing town.

But the Garlands soon discovered that it took money to live in Petersburg, too, and to be socially accepted. They did not fit in with the gentry, so Hugh Garland moved his family again, this time to St. Louis, Missouri, a town of seventy-eight thousand people. St. Louis had scores of shops, restaurants, fancy hotels, and a steady influx of travelers from all over the world who came in steamboats to the town's levees.

The move was a stroke of luck for Lizzy, though she didn't know it at the time. There was a sizable black population in St. Louis, many of them women and many of them free. On the streets, shopping for the family, Lizzy ran into these free black women. Though many were domestics, a good number were professionals: midwives, nurses, even doctors, keepers of taverns and cook shops.

With a young son to consider, Lizzy began to truly think about her own freedom, and that of her son's.

She did not want her darling boy to be a slave to anybody.

Established in a small law firm, Garland was not doing well and as always, needed money. So he decided to hire out some of his slaves.

He wanted to hire out Aggy, Lizzy's mother, but Lizzy intervened, saying that her mother was too old and that she herself had all the skills of a seamstress and could certainly bring in a goodly amount of money. Garland agreed. So did Betty Burwell, Garland's sister, who, on marrying Mr. E. P. Putnam of Pittsburgh, became Lizzy's legal mistress. And so, for the next twelve years Lizzy sewed for the white gentry, helped to make contacts by the Garlands' connections. The ladies for whom she sewed quickly recommended her as being especially talented, polite, genteel, trustworthy, and responsible.

Lizzy sewed everything for wives of rich husbands, from exquisite breakfast robes to walking dresses to dinner gowns. Soon she was regarded as the very best in her profession. And the money she made she gave to Garland.

With her earnings she was supporting seventeen people in the Garland household, and she still performed all her domestic duties as well.

She was now thirty-two years old and very pleasant to look at. In this time she met a man named James Keckley whose acquaintance she'd once made in Petersburg. He asked her to marry him, but Lizzy refused. She first wanted to be free, because James Keckley was free. She was afraid he'd grow frustrated with her still in bondage and abandon her. Or worse yet, want to leave St. Louis with her and she could not.

So she approached Hugh Garland with the idea of buying her own freedom and that of her son's.

Garland refused. But Lizzy knew he could always use the money, so she kept after him from time to time until he finally said yes. She could buy her freedom and that of her son's for $1,200, an enormous sum at that time.

Encouraged that she would someday be free, Lizzy Hobbs married James Keckley in 1852. The wedding took place in the Garlands' parlor and was attended by the whole family and many friends.

After marriage, Lizzy's husband was discovered not to be a free man after all, and even to possibly being a runaway.

And he drank heavily. They lived together for eight years and after their separation, as always, Lizzy kept on as a seamstress and continued working in the Garland household.

In spring of 1854, Hugh Garland died and Anne's brother, Armistead Burwell Jr., came to help settle matters. He was a successful lawyer and planter and Lizzy approached him with her proposal to be free. He was also her half brother. He was, as Lizzy tells us, "a kind-hearted man."

He agreed, as did Anne, to honor Hugh Garland's word. Lizzy made $3 a day as a seamstress. On the advice of people she knew she decided to go to New York, where it would be easier to raise the money. But as she was readying to leave, Anne Garland told her that before she could go she had to have six names of responsible people who could make up the loss if Lizzy did not come back.

Lizzy got five names and could get no more. She was already cast down and weeping when a Mrs. Le Bourgois came to the house and offered to raise the money for her. She had heard of Lizzy's plight and felt terrible for her.

The $1,200 was raised and on November 13, 1855, Anne Garland signed the papers making Lizzy Keckley free, as well as her son George, "a bright mulatto."

George was now sixteen years old, almost white, and his mother had saved him from a lifetime of slavery.

Lizzy decided that her next move would be to go to Washington City. Before she left she paid the money for her freedom back to Mrs. Le Bourgois, in full.

LIZZY KECKLEY CAME to Washington without a husband and penniless. Soon she was making $2.50 a day, sewing for many kind and wealthy ladies who were the cream of American society. She had enrolled her son, George, in Wilberforce University in Ohio, a school for blacks that was full of the mixed-race children of white planters.

One of Lizzy's foremost employers in Washington was the wife of Colonel Robert E. Lee, of the distinguished Lee family. Lee would someday become the commander of Virginia's defenses in the American Civil War. His wife, Mary, was the great-granddaughter of Martha Washington. In the fall of 1860, a dress Lizzy made for Colonel Lee's wife was so admired that Lizzy soon had other important customers, like Mrs. Mathilda Emory of Texas; Mrs. Margaretta Hetzel of Virginia; and Mrs. Varina Davis, whose husband, Jefferson, would soon become president of the Confederate States of America.

Lizzy sewed for Varina Davis's children as well. And when the Union started to tear apart after the election of Abraham Lincoln as president, the Davises were all set to return South and leave Washington. Varina Davis asked Lizzy to go with them.

"I will take good care of you," she told Lizzy. "When war breaks out, the colored people will suffer in the North because they will be blamed for being the cause of the war."

Lizzy thought the matter over seriously. But she knew the North was strong and right, so she decided to stay in Washington City.

ONE DAY AS she was sewing in her rented Twelfth Street house, Lizzy was visited by a woman named Mrs. Margaret McLean, one of her patrons. She had been invited to dinner at Willard's, the exclusive hotel in Washington. The date was the following Sunday and she needed a dress. Willard's was the place to be seen.

"You must commence to work on it right away," she told Lizzy, who told her she had more work promised now than she could deliver.

Mrs. McLean wouldn't take no as an answer. "I have often heard it said that you wanted to sew for ladies in the White House. Well, I have it in my power to obtain for you this privilege. I know Mrs. Lincoln well."

Right about then Lizzy employed some helpers to work on the dress for Mrs. McLean. Sometime during the next week, Mary Lincoln spilled coffee on an expensive lavender gown she hoped to wear to a party. Distraught, she did not know what to do until Mrs. McLean told her about Elizabeth Keckley.

When Lizzy delivered Mrs. McLean's dress to her at Willard's, Mrs. McLean told her to go upstairs to parlor number six, where she would meet Mary Lincoln. "She may find use for you yet," Mrs. McLean said.

And so Elizabeth Keckley went upstairs in Willard's to parlor number six, where she met Mary Lincoln, who told her to come to the White House the next morning for an interview.

Epilogue

MARY LINCOLN GOT her bright rose-colored moiré antique gown in time for her party. And she also got herself a best friend in Elizabeth Keckley, though she did not know it at the time. Lizzy not only delivered the gown on time, she helped Mary Lincoln dress and did her hair as well.

That spring Lizzy made about sixteen dresses for Mary Lincoln. And when the president's wife went to Long Branch, New Jersey, on vacation that summer of 1861, Lizzy sewed for other important wives, like Mrs. Secretary Welles, Mrs. Secretary Stanton, and other wives of cabinet members.

It soon became known that Lizzy Keckley was the "only person in Washington who could get along with Mary Lincoln when she went into a frenzy about people maligning her or her husband's name."

Lizzy fit in with the staff of the Lincoln White House, too, even though color discrimination existed "below-stairs." Most of the staff were the mixed-race children of slaves, and when Abraham Lincoln brought his valet from

Springfield along into the president's mansion, the man left in two days, feeling the disdain of the servants because of his dark skin color.

As for "above-stairs," Mary Lincoln was soon sharing secrets with Lizzy and asking her advice about social problems.

In the outside world Lizzy was approached because of her position in the Lincoln family circle. She was asked to make connections for many people. For a fee, naturally. She turned down all such offers, in one instance an offer of several thousand dollars.

"Sooner than betray the trust of a friend," she said, "I would throw myself in the Potomac River."

MEANWHILE, THE WAR was progressing. Mary Lincoln's own brother, George, fought for the South as did three of her half brothers. She was criticized for that and when torn in pieces over it, it was Lizzy who comforted her.

Then Emilie, Mary's "Little Sister," as the president called her, came for a visit and the Northern newspapers criticized Mary Lincoln for "having Southern spies in the White House." Indeed, *Harper's Weekly* described all of Mary's sisters as "the toast of Southerners."

The Northern papers even labeled Mary Lincoln a "Southern sympathizer" and ran stories about her sister Emilie smuggling supplies across lines to the South. At the same time the Southern papers accused her of being a traitor to her roots. Mary wept. Lizzy was there to comfort her.

Mary Lincoln, wanting to escape the White House at times, began walking the one-third mile to Lizzy's rented rooms to be fitted for her gowns. Fashion was almost a god with her and she made many demands on Lizzy. Accustomed to dealing with difficult white mistresses, Lizzy managed always to oblige and soothe her.

In turn, Mary found herself turning to Lizzy in difficult times, much as she used to depend on her Mammy Sally as a child. And when she was not unburdening herself on Lizzy, she was shopping to relieve her anxieties about the war, about being left out of politics in that male-run world, about important Washington matrons snubbing her, and about criticism in the newspapers.

She had discovered, her first year in the White House, that there was a $20,000 congressional allowance given to each new administration for repairs on the White House. And she shopped—in New York, in Philadelphia, and from Paris—to accumulate goods to make up for the disappointments in her life.

Soon the $20,000 was gone and there was more public criticism of her extravagance. So, in a vicious circle, she would have more gowns made to appease her vanity and restore her confidence.

By now she and Lizzy were confidantes. "I must dress in costly materials because the people scrutinize every article I wear," she told Lizzy. "The very fact of coming from the West subjects me to more searching observation."

BECAUSE HER PERSONAL finances improved and her reputation grew, Lizzy was able to open workrooms across from her apartment and hire apprentices. Then, in mid-August she was notified of the death of her son, George, who had left Wilberforce to enlist in the Union Army. He had to enlist as a white man if he wanted to fight, because blacks at the time were allowed only to dig fortifications and cook. He enlisted as George W. D. Kirkland in the First Missouri Volunteers and he fell in his first fight—the Battle at Wilson's Creek in southern Missouri. Mary Lincoln, in New York at the time, wrote her friend Lizzy a long letter of comfort.

BY THIS TIME Lizzy was fully involved with the Lincoln family. She helped care for and quiet the rowdy boys, Willie and Tad. She stayed with Mary when the woman came down with one of her now-frequent migraines. She even, on occasion, combed the president's hair. The Lincolns did not consider her a stranger but spoke freely in front of her, even if they argued. In particular, Lizzy was privy to the argument they had when Lincoln discovered that his wife was over budget by nearly $7,000 on the household yearly allowance.

The beginning of 1862 was not good in the White House. Lincoln was upset by his wife's extravagance, and twelve-year-old Willie was fearfully sick.

SICKNESS IN THOSE DAYS was not to be taken lightly. In Victorian times parents intentionally had many children because they knew that one episode of cholera or typhoid or scarlet fever could wipe out a family. There were no antibiotics, no aspirin, no drugs of any kind, and medical knowledge, too, was sorely lacking. And so, when Willie came down with his fever, the Lincolns had every right to be fearful.

Willie likely had typhoid fever. His parents watched him helplessly for weeks, while he worsened and finally died on February 20, 1862.

Lizzy was there with the Lincolns through the terrible ordeal. She was witness to Abraham Lincoln's weeping and was "awestruck" at seeing so powerful a man reduced to tears.

Mary Lincoln would not be consoled. This was the second son she had lost. She had frequent crying jags. She came down with her headaches. And Lizzy was there to comfort and to listen.

"Willie would have been the hope and stay of my old age," she told Lizzy, who had, herself, counted on the same thing from her own son.

Deep depression settled over Mary Lincoln and the only cheer she found was in ordering expensive mourning gowns from Lizzy and black-veiled bonnets from New York. She locked herself in her room to get away from the rest of the world. Lincoln was too overwhelmed himself to attend her. It could be said that Lizzy Keckley and Mary Todd were drawn even closer in mourning Willie because Lizzy understood, having lost her own son.

As if she were not busy enough that summer, Lizzy founded a relief society to raise money to care for the contrabands (former slaves) who were living in great numbers and in abject poverty in Washington at the time. She fell back on her church and her many friends, black and white, to raise the money to help these people. Of them, she said, "Poor dusky children of slavery, men and women of my own race, the transition from slavery to freedom was too much for you." She even traveled to New York and Boston to raise money for her cause.

LIZZY WAS IN THE PRESENCE of the Lincolns in the White House one day when Abraham led Mary over to a window and pointed across the Potomac to an insane hospital. He told his wife that if she let her grief and depression take over she would soon be insane and she would have to go there.

By the time 1862 ended, Mary Lincoln's fog of mourning had somewhat lifted. The war and life as she'd known it were going on without her. Lincoln had already issued a proclamation freeing all of Washington, D.C.'s slaves and now the tide of public opinion was in favor of emancipation for all of them.

The blacks could only hope. Then, on January 1, 1863, Lincoln signed the Emancipation Proclamation, freeing all of the slaves.

Lizzy finally felt herself equal and saw the world differently now, while all Mary Lincoln could feel was a renewed sense of loss "for life as we have known it."

Still in mourning, she had, with Lizzy's help, sought out mediums (spiritualists) and claimed to have learned "wonderful things about Willie" in the séances those mediums conducted. Both she and Lizzy took part in the séances, seeking relief from past sufferings.

By fall of 1863 Mary Lincoln had lost three half brothers in the war. All had fought for the South. But Mary refused to mourn them because "in fighting against the North they have fought against me and my husband."

Eighteen sixty-four was an election year, and Mary came out of her mourning for Willie by entertaining lavishly. Naturally, she needed many new gowns, and she went on more shopping sprees, accumulating thousands of dollars of debt. Lincoln was unaware of her debt, but Lizzy knew of it. And so Mary drew Lizzy even more into her confidence.

Before the election, Lizzy asked Mary Lincoln if she could have "the right-hand glove that the President wears at the first public reception after his second inaugural."

Lincoln did win a second term, defeating one of his former generals, George B. McClellan. The war was coming to an end now, and in April of 1865 Lizzy went along on a boat and train trip with Mary and her husband, up the James River to City Point, Petersburg, and Richmond, Virginia. President Jefferson Davis, head of the Confederacy, had fled Richmond, and it was in ruins. But what most moved Lizzy was Petersburg, where she had once lived as a slave for the Garlands. She was nostalgic, proud, and bitter all at the same time.

She had come far, she knew, and so had the race to whom she belonged. After the president's first public reception, following the inaugural, Lizzy got the president's white right-hand glove and treasured it always.

AFTER LINCOLN'S ASSASSINATION Mary Lincoln stayed in the White House for six more weeks, refusing to move out. The new president, Andrew Johnson, stayed in a house on Fifteenth and Eighth streets and did not push her. Mary Lincoln was often uncontrollable in her grief and refused to face the world. Lizzy and twelve-year-old Tad slept in the same room with her.

Lincoln's body was returned to Illinois, but Mary would not make the trip for the burial. Robert had to take over. Everyone wanted her to go back to Illinois to live, but she said no; it held too many memories for her.

Finally, with the persuasion of Robert, now twenty-two, she packed up to leave the White House, taking five years' worth of gifts she had received as First Lady, even though technically they were not hers. She had decided to go and live in Chicago. In packing she gave away all of Lincoln's things. His hat, his cane, even his shawl, she gave to White House aides. To Lizzy she gave his comb and brush, a pair of his overshoes, and the cloak she was wearing when her husband was shot.

Late in May of 1865 Mary Lincoln, Lizzy, Tad, and Robert took the train to Chicago where they took some rooms in a hotel. Robert entered a law firm. Lizzy stayed in Chicago only two weeks because Mary Lincoln could no longer afford to pay her and she wanted to reopen her shop in Washington, which had been neglected. Back in Washington she bandied it about that Mary Lincoln "was practicing the closest economy" in her style of living.

Mary and Lizzy did not see each other again for two years. Mary had asked Congress for money. She hoped for $100,000, which represented her husband's salary had he finished out his term in office.

Lizzy made a trip to Virginia to see the Garlands, who gave her a joyful welcome. "Even to a slave," she said, "the past is dear." Many ex-slaves at the time were visiting old masters and having reconciliations with their former owners.

The two women, bonded by good times and bad times, stayed in touch and saw each other again over the years. In Lizzy Keckley, Mary Lincoln seemed to have found her "Mammy Sally" again and, indeed, turned to her in all her hours of need and loneliness.

As for Lizzy Keckley, she recognized what she had in the friendship. She perhaps saw in Mary her own white heritage, although she did not need it to continue leading a productive and happy life. She had her memories to carry her through lonely hours: the time spent on the Burwell plantation; her time with Robert and his wife and children; her rising above the status that whites in her life always wanted her to be satisfied with; and the knowledge that along the way she had purchased her own freedom, given a son to "the cause," known a president and his family, helped start an organization in Washington, D.C., to help the freedman, and been a solid and continuing presence in so many lives, both black and white.

Author's Note

I HAVE ALWAYS BEEN FASCINATED with the tale of Elizabeth Keckley, the black woman born into slavery, who grew up in bondage and eventually purchased her own freedom and that of her son's.

The fact that she ended up in the White House, a personal dressmaker and confidante of Mary Lincoln, that the two women became fast friends, further intrigued me.

In looking at their childhoods, I thought: How utterly different. One a slave girl, mistreated and overworked; the other the daughter of a wealthy and influential family in Lexington, Kentucky, herself surrounded by slaves.

The idea presented itself. Why not explore the childhoods of each of these women who were buffeted by the turmoil of their times, whose mettle was tested every day? As I began to research the idea, it loomed even stronger.

I have depicted Mary Lincoln's childhood with as much accuracy as possible. A writer need not have to stray far from the truth to make an interesting story here. It had all the ingredients of a good novel, right down to the "evil" stepmother. I have had to, for the sake of story, invent some scenes and piece together others, for frequently in research, the pieces don't always fit.

But other pieces stand firm under the test of time. For instance, Mary Todd always did want to live in the White House and marry a president. She did get put into Ward's girls' school by her parents, and her Grandma Parker did live "up the hill" and refuse to accept the Todd girls' stepmother, Betsy. Grandfather Levi Todd's wife, Jane, did fashion a wedding dress from weeds and wild flax, and the incident about Mary Todd desperately wanting a hoopskirt, and of Betsy's disapproval, is true.

Liz Humphreys did come to stay and go to school with Mary.

Mammy Sally did have a sign painted on the fence to welcome runaways, and Mary Todd did find out about it and was a staunch supporter of the practice. Elizabeth, Mary's older sister, did invite her younger sister to Springfield, Illinois, to "stay a while," and both Frances and Mary Todd met their husbands that way.

It is a bit murky about what troubled George, Mary's brother, christened George Rogers Clark, but I have it down as an early drinking problem combined with feeling guilty because their mother died at his birth. (Having been in George's position, with my mother dying at my birth, I can relate to George's guilt, which only deepens, instead of lessens, as one grows older and begins to comprehend the full extent of what a mother's death means.)

It is also true that when she was older and went to Mentelle's School for Young Ladies, Mary Todd was fetched home only on weekends, making her feel even more alienated from her family. So it wasn't difficult for her to give up the ghost and go to Springfield, Illinois, to her sister Elizabeth's house when the time came for her to leave home.

What did I learn upon researching the childhood of Mary Todd? That her life was filled with a sense of loss (right down to the middle name—Ann—that was taken from her when a young sister was born and given the name) even before she married Abraham Lincoln. I learned that she was completely dependent upon their black nanny, Mammy Sally, to make things right when they went wrong. And so, in later years turned to Elizabeth Keckley, the black dressmaker, when she was hurting or worried.

I learned that when she was excessively worried, or feeling abandoned (as when her young husband went riding circuit as a lawyer), she turned to shopping to make her feel better.

When she got to be First Lady, there were plenty of occasions upon which she felt abandoned or at a sense of loss. And so, as First Lady, she shopped, excessively, and ran up a score of bills while in the White House.

But all the troubles Mary Todd had when she was a child, whether real or imagined, cannot be compared to those of Elizabeth Keckley.

It is true that Elizabeth was started on chores at about

age four. And that she was cruelly whipped for trying to pick up the baby of the master's house, with a fireplace shovel.

Her half brother, Robert Burwell of Dinwiddie County, Virginia, did become her master and treated her with cruel indifference, even "farming" her out to the "slave breaker" next door in order to break her spirit.

It would not be broken. She had an indomitable spirit, and eventually both the slave breaker and Robert begged her forgiveness for their treatment of her.

The stories of other slaves being sold as children, of Jane being made to eat worms, only touch the surface of the mistreatment of slaves. And while most slaves were broken by such treatment, Elizabeth Keckley was only made stronger.

She did sew enough and work enough to support the whole family when she was grown. She did buy her own freedom and came to be known as a source of strength to many white people around her.

It is a fact, though surprising, that she was asked to be in the wedding party of several white girls. Research tells us this. Apparently the custom was practiced in the South, especially when the girl was as attractive and poised as Elizabeth Keckley.

Her dressmaking, soon recognized by the likes of Mrs. Jefferson Davis, wife of the future president of the Confederacy, was enviable, to say the least. All the cream of society had to have one of her dresses.

So, once ensconced in Washington City, she had a

whole list of wealthy patrons, and just about that time Mary Lincoln came to play her part as First Lady. The rest is a wonderful, heartbreaking, true story.

I hope I have done it justice. The tale of this friendship between these two women is remarkable, indeed.

Bibliography

Baker, Jean H. *Mary Todd Lincoln, A Biography.* New York: W. W. Norton & Company, Ltd., 1987.

Fleischner, Jennifer. *Mrs. Lincoln and Mrs. Keckly, The Remarkable Story of the Friendship Between a First Lady and a Former Slave.* New York: Broadway Books, a Division of Random House, 2003.

Keckley, Elizabeth. *Behind the Scenes, or Thirty Years a Slave and Four Years in the White House.* New York: Oxford University Press, 1988.

Leech, Margaret. *Reveille in Washington 1860–1865.* New York: Harper & Bros., 1941.

Lewis, Lloyd. *The Assassination of Lincoln: History and Myth.* Lincoln, NE: University of Nebraska Press, 1957.

Morrow, Honore. *Great Captain.* New York: William Morrow and Company, 1930.

Robertson, David. *Booth.* New York: Doubleday & Company, 1998.

Reader Chat Page

1. Thinking about their respective childhoods, what experiences might have set the stage for the fast friendship Mary and Lizzy form as adults?

2. As children, Mary dreams of living in the White House, and Lizzy dreams of buying her own freedom. Lizzy's Grandma says, "First you grow up . . . And then if'n you still want it bad enough, you'll find a way to do it." What steps can you, the reader, take to make your dreams come true?

3. After she paints flowers on the fence surrounding the family's house, Mary lies to her stepmother, saying she did it to make the fence prettier. In fact, the flower painting was a sign for runaway slaves. What might have inspired her to want to help, when at this time in American history, many people saw nothing wrong with slavery?

4. In the White House, Mary is known for her excessive spending habits. Why do you think shopping becomes such a habit for her? What do you do to cope when you've had a tough day?

5. Even at four-years-old, Lizzy's half-siblings and fellow slaves harass her, saying she gets special treatment as the master's daughter. How does the fact that she doesn't fit in work to Lizzy's advantage?

6. Uncle Raymond kills himself rather than be punished by Massa for losing a harness. What was he trying to communicate by doing this? What would you have done if you were in his place?

7. When Lizzy is loaned out to Mr. Bingham, what about Lizzy's behavior makes him cry and vow to never beat her again? Do you think he continues to beat other slaves?

8. Why do you think Lizzy's brother, Robert, doesn't protect her from Master Kirkland?

9. Slavery was once legal in this country. Are there any laws in contemporary America that you consider to be equally unjust and that violate human rights?